THE LEGACY SERIES

SERIES TITLES

Trust Issues
K.P. Davis

We Should Be Somewhere by Now
Stephen Tuttle

Burner and Other Stories
Katrina Denza

The Plan of Chicago
Barry Pearce

The Caged Man
Calvin Mills

A Day Doesn't Go By When I Don't Have Regrets
J. Malcolm Garcia

These Are My People
Steve Fox

Adult Children
Laurence Klavan

Guardians & Saints
Diane Josefowicz

Western Terminus: Stories and A Novella
Michael Keefe

Like Human
Janet Goldberg

The Hopefuls
Elizabeth Oness

Never Stop Exiting
Michael Hopkins

Broken Heart Syndrome
Anne Colwell

The Mexican Messiah: A Novella & Stories
Jay Kauffmann

Close to a Flame
Colleen Alles

American Animism
Jamey Gallagher

Keeping What's Best Left Kept Secret
David Ricchiute

Soaked
Toby LeBlanc

The Path of Totality
Marie Zhuikov

Shocker in Gloomtown
Dan Libman

The Continental Divide
Bob Johnson

The Three Devils and Other Stories
William Luvaas

The Correct Response
Manfred Gabriel

Welcome Back to the World: A Novella & Stories
Rob Davidson

Greyhound Cowboy and Other Stories
Ken Post

Close Call
Kim Suhr

The Waterman
Gary Schanbacher

Signs of the Imminent Apocalypse and Other Stories
Heidi Bell

What We Might Become
Sara Reish Desmond

The Silver State Stories
Michael Darcher

An Instinct for Movement
Michael Mattes

The Machine We Trust
Tim Conrad

Gridlock
Brett Biebel

Salt Folk
Ryan Habermeyer

The Commission of Inquiry
Patrick Nevins

Maximum Speed
Kevin Clouther

Reach Her in This Light
Jane Curtis

The Spirit in My Shoes
John Michael Cummings

The Effects of Urban Renewal on Mid-Century America and Other Crime Stories
Jeff Esterholm

What Makes You Think You're Supposed to Feel Better
Jody Hobbs Hesler

Fugitive Daydreams
Leah McCormack

Hoist House: A Novella & Stories
Jenny Robertson

Finding the Bones: Stories & A Novella
Nikki Kallio

Self-Defense
Corey Mertes

Where Are Your People From?
James B. De Monte

Sometimes Creek
Steve Fox

The Plagues
Joe Baumann

The Clayfields
Elise Gregory

Kind of Blue
Christopher Chambers

Evangelina Everyday
Dawn Burns

Township
Jamie Lyn Smith

Responsible Adults
Patricia Ann McNair

Great Escapes from Detroit
Joseph O'Malley

Nothing to Lose
Kim Suhr

The Appointed Hour
Susanne Davis

TRUST ISSUES

stories

K.P. DAVIS

CORNERSTONE PRESS
UNIVERSITY OF WISCONSIN-STEVENS POINT

Cornerstone Press, Stevens Point, Wisconsin 54481
Copyright © 2025 Kimberly Parish Davis
www.uwsp.edu/cornerstone

Printed in the United States of America by
Point Print and Design Studio, Stevens Point, Wisconsin

Library of Congress Control Number: 2025943471
ISBN: 978-1-968148-14-0

This is a work of fiction. Names, characters, businesses, places, events, and incidents are either the products of the author's imagination or used in a fictitious manner. Any resemblance to actual persons, living or dead, or actual events is purely coincidental.

Cornerstone Press titles are produced in courses and internships offered by the Department of English at the University of Wisconsin–Stevens Point.

DIRECTOR & PUBLISHER
Dr. Ross K. Tangedal

EXECUTIVE EDITORS
Jeff Snowbarger, Freesia McKee

EDITORIAL DIRECTOR
Brett Hill

SENIOR EDITORS
Paige Biever, Eva Nielsen, Reilly Crous

PRESS STAFF
Karlie Harpold, Lilly Kulbeck, Jacob Childress, Sam Zajkowski, Kimberly Janesch, Samantha Bjork, Sophie McPherson, Madison Schultz, Autumn Vine

For Bill Davis, my rock.

Nell

If you could have gotten her to talk about herself at all, Nell would have given her stepdad, Gilbert, the credit for making her the woman she became. No telling what her life might have been like if she and Susan Jenkins hadn't gotten caught kissing. They were in the powder room at the home of a two-year-old Nell was supposed to have been babysitting. Nell was fourteen, and Susan, who lived in the same apartment complex, had invited herself over. They'd polished off most of a bottle of peppermint schnapps after tasting everything in the liquor cabinet, and the two of them, drunk as lords, were sporting hickeys when the child's parents came home.

The apartment complex seemed nice with its trendy silver wallpaper in the bathrooms and its community gym beside the pool. The adjoining woods with suspended walkways crisscrossing back and forth across Buffalo Bayou looked like the perfect place for kids to run and play. That's what it looked like, but the adults who lived there were oblivious to what went on among the teens skulking out to the woods after dark to smoke weed, drink Boons Farm wine, and feel each other up.

When Gilbert heard about the babysitting debacle, the dyke jokes made dinner unbearable. "Nelly won't be having any of that pecan pie you made, Mother. She's allergic to nuts!" Or when Nell had a cold, "Take a dose of that Dyquil. It's formulated especially for people like you." Or worst of all, "What do you call a lesbian with fat fingers? Well-hung!"

Nell's mother would eventually say, "Gilbert! That is enough of that nasty talk at the table." She rarely joined the dinner conversation, preferring to read her bosom-heaver novels and smoke through the meal. Listening wasn't her strong suit.

Nell was mortified by Gilbert's rude jokes. Sex was a taboo subject in her mind, and she barely even knew what a lesbian was. In her experience, people only ever whispered that word. To her, it was about the worst thing you could call a girl. Besides, Nell liked boys. She'd rather play with Legos with her boy cousins than dolls with the silly girls. Kissing Susan Jenkins had been on account of the booze. They weren't hot for each other—that'd be weird—but Gilbert would not let it alone, so Nell took to gobbling her dinner and escaping to her room as quickly as possible.

Gilbert also started leaving the bathroom door open when he peed and wandering around naked at night. He must have enjoyed Nell's horrified expression, because "coinci-dental" embarrassing encounters seemed to happen more frequently. Nell couldn't understand how her mother failed to notice, but she never was there when it happened. Nell sometimes woke up in the night to see Gilbert standing in her doorway. She'd lay stiff as a board willing him to go away as she tried to breathe like a sleeping person. She only dared to look directly at him one time when a full moon beamed through the window silhouetting his slow-moving hand on his protruding thing. It terrified her. She recalled a story from a *Penthouse* magazine she found in Gilbert's underwear drawer about a woman who saved herself from a rapist by yanking the cord out of her bedside lamp to electrocute her attacker. Nell imagined how hard it would be to rip the cord loose from her lamp while fighting Gilbert—all 300 pounds of him. Even in her imagination, it never worked out. She just dropped the lamp and broke it while Gilbert squashed her into submission.

Nell was sixteen when her mother and Gilbert came in drunk one night. She could hear them fumbling to unlock the door. One of them leaned on the doorbell a few times before Nell let them in. Her mother stumbled off to bed while Gilbert went to pee. Nell was getting a drink of water in the kitchen when Gilbert wandered in. He had on his starched white shirt and tie and a pair of black dress socks, but his pants and shoes were gone. He opened the refrigerator door and stood there scratching his balls.

Nell said, "Oh my *God*, Gilbert!" She'd have been okay if she'd stopped there, but she went on. "Your turkey's not looking very wild now, is he?" She knew it was a mistake the minute she said it and turned to make a hasty retreat, but Gilbert leapt at her, grabbing a handful of her hair and slamming her face down onto the breakfast table. He pulled up her nightshirt and smeared butter from the dish on the table on her and then on himself before he shoved his now erect penis into her.

"My turkey's been wanting to show you what *real* sex feels like." He growled and wheezed in her ear.

The sex hurt, just like she'd heard it would, but she couldn't focus on that because he mashed her head so tight against the table she expected it to burst like a watermelon. Screaming was impossible. Each of Gilbert's thrusts felt like he was ripping her guts open and knocked a little more wind out of her.

He moaned when he came after five mighty thrusts, then he stood back and wiped his dick on a dishtowel which he carefully folded and draped over the oven door handle. "Not a damn thing wrong with my turkey," he said, chuckling as he strolled off to bed.

Nell's thoughts from then on revolved around getting away and never having to see Gilbert again. Gilbert, meanwhile, acted like it never happened—or like he didn't remember it because he was so drunk. One night at dinner, though, he let the façade slip. "Ummmm-mm. Butter that potato, mother, and slide some pork right in there," he said. Shirley had her back turned, serving the plates at the stove. When he winked at her, Nell decided she had to tell someone.

It was a week before she finally got a chance to talk to her mother without Gilbert around. "Gilbert raped me." They were standing by the harvest gold washer and dryer folding clothes.

Shirley whipped around, scrunched her eyebrows together, and pressed her lips into a thin line. She glowered at her one and only daughter for an eternity. Eventually, she spat out a string of words like they were poison: "You are an evil child. What won't you say to hurt him? Gilbert is a good Christian man. He would never, *could* never think of doing any such thing."

Nell's mouth dropped open. "You think I'm lying?"

Shirley narrowed her eyes but said nothing.

"When you came in drunk from the Keller's party. He nearly suffocated me holding me down right there." She pointed at the table.

"Stop. That is disgusting. I won't listen to your wild stories."

"I'm not making it up!" Nell's throat clamped shut and she felt hot, angry tears sting her eyes. She wanted to tell her mother about Gilbert looking at her when she slept, but the words wouldn't come. She threw the T-shirt she'd been folding into the laundry basket and stormed out of the kitchen.

"Young lady! You had better get back in here."

Nell kept going, slamming her bedroom door so hard the pictures shook on the walls.

"You're grounded!" Shirley shouted after her.

That Sunday after church, Shirley dragged Nell through the dark corridor behind the sanctuary to the pastor's office. The smarmy man with his greasy pompadour was hanging his robes in the closet. He had on so much cologne it was hard for Nell to pay attention to anything else.

"Nell, your mother tells me you've been confused lately."

"Confused?" Nell asked.

"I just want you to understand it's normal at your age to have questions about sex, but that if we trust in the Lord, all things will be revealed in their own good time."

"What are you talking about?"

"I'd like you to pray with me."

"What did my mother tell you? Did she tell you Gilbert raped me?"

That's when the preacher slapped his hand on Nell's forehead and raised his face to toward the ceiling shouting, "Dear Heavenly Father, we beseech you to heal this young woman . . ."

And that's as far as he got. Nell knocked her chair over getting out of there. From that point on, church was a place she went on Wednesday nights only. She told her mother she was going to Youth Alive, but she never left the parking lot where she drank beer and smoked weed with the "bad kids."

Then Nell got her driver's license, and her dumbass parents gave her a car to drive so they wouldn't have to drive her around anymore. It meant she wasn't stuck with the same scumbags around the apartments, and while there was no one at school she'd miss, she was too smart to just run away. She needed a diploma and a plan, so she spent her last semester of high school going to classes in the mornings and driving all over town delivering airline tickets for a travel agency in the afternoons.

Nell lucked out on the car. It'd been her uncle-who-died's car. Her grandparents had it out in an old shed, and they'd been glad to get rid of the 1969 El Camino with its 454 cubic inch engine. It looked like hell on the outside, with dings and scratches and blistered paint on top, but it was scary fast. Her family couldn't have known anything about it, or they'd never have let a sixteen-year-old brand new driver get behind the wheel. She called it Broomstick. She thought she was clever saying, "Let's fly, Broomstick!" She didn't have many repeat passengers after they rode with her. Broomstick could do zero to sixty in the blink of an eye. Nell would pick up her airline tickets for the afternoon, smoke a joint, and hit the road. She had stops all over the greater Houston area, and a lot of times that meant going way south on the Gulf Freeway. There was nobody on that road but truckers at two o'clock in the afternoon, and Nell would get on the C.B. radio as she turned south and say, "Breaker, breaker-one-nine, good buddy. Just Broomstick flying by. What's the smokey report?" She'd work out where the cops were and put her foot down twisting and weaving around the trucks on the road in front of her. She occasionally got up to 120, but she liked to cruise at about ninety. She figured if she ever got caught, they wouldn't just arrest her, they'd put her under the jail. She liked the feeling it gave her knowing she was an outlaw. She never got caught, often making the fifty miles to Galveston in well under forty minutes.

After Gilbert, that car was the second greatest influence in Nell's young life.

Nell's parents didn't worry about her when she was out. They never even noticed she was gone. She was free to become. Of course, she was also free to pay the maintenance costs on her car, and that's how she met Marlon. He was a hippie mechanic with a bald spot and scraggly blond hair that hung down past his shoulders. He was about seven feet tall, and he made pot cookies that would knock you out. His place, on the way to the Ship Channel, had a dilapidated garage and a peer-and-beam shack of a house. It was sand-wiched between warehouses at the end of a long oyster shell driveway lined with broken-down cars and miscellaneous vehicles. Nell's first glimpse of the place was from the pas-senger seat of Marlon's wrecker as he towed Broomstick to the garage.

He said, "It's not much, but it's home."

Nell just stared at him. The guy was kind of freaky, but not in a scary way. He just looked odd. She'd been deep in thought trying to work out how she was going to get Broom-stick rolling as fast as possible and get home. She'd had to walk about a mile with her thumb out before anybody came along. She finally got a ride to a service station where the guy gave her Marlon's number after Gilbert hung up on her.

As Marlon lowered Broomstick onto the driveway, Nell asked, "Is there a bus service way out here?"

Marlon laughed. "Bus service! Good one. No, man, but we'll get you back on the road this afternoon. I know these El Caminos—got a lot of spare parts."

"I'm broke," she said.

The gangly man smiled and tilted his head. "Don't sweat it," he said. "We'll work something out."

Nell pulled a J from her purse. "You mind if I light up?"

"Not as long as you pass it my way."

Marlon did know what was wrong with Broomstick, and he had the parts to fix it. Part of the deal he worked out with Nell was that she had to hang out with him while he worked. He liked to talk, and Nell steered the talk to explanations of what he was doing. It just made sense that she got up under the car with him and started cranking a wrench herself.

Broomstick had been rode hard and put up wet, as the cowboys liked to say, so she broke down with some frequency. It meant Nell started spending a lot of time at Marlon's tinkering and tuning.

"Nelly girl, you're becoming a true shade-tree mechanic," Marlon said as he passed her a joint one evening. She looked a mess, with grease on her face, in her hair, and down the front of her T-shirt. Her hands and forearms were the only clean parts showing since she'd scrubbed them with scratchy Lava soap. Marlon, by contrast, looked like he was ready to go to town. It was a bright April evening. Not too hot, not too cold, and they were sitting on folding lawn chairs on Marlon's one patch of grass in front of the house.

"I didn't think I'd ever get the timing adjusted right," Nell said.

"I told you—you have to use your eyes *and* your ears. There's an art to it—like tuning a musical instrument."

"I'm not very musical, Marlon!" She coughed on the exhale and they both laughed.

"So, you're fixin' to graduate, huh?"

"Don't remind me."

"Why not?"

"I don't know what's going to happen next."

"You apply to college?"

"No." Nell tucked her chin and shook her head.

"Why not?"

"Don't want to. Fed up with school." She sucked a deep drag on the joint.

"You go to college, there'd be a dormitory," Marlon said.

"Nah. I don't even know what I'd study."

"So, you need a job."

"I have a job."

"No, I mean a job that pays you enough to live on."

"I'm good—almost $400 in the bank."

Marlon pursed his lips. "Have you checked out what apartments cost? That's like one month's rent."

"Right, so I'm good."

"No . . . you need $800 to get in the door. You pay the first and last month up front."

Nell rolled that around in her head for a minute. "That's bullshit."

"And how you planning to eat?" Marlon continued, gathering a head of steam.

"With a knife and fork." Nell squeezed her elbows against her sides defensively and sat back as she said it.

Marlon softened his voice and leaned back as well. "No," he said, "I mean, does that little delivery job earn you enough to buy food *and* pay rent?"

"Well, no. I figured I'd have to probably get a full-time job somewhere." Nell's voice got smaller as the enormity of it all settled around her.

Marlon reached over and touched a clean patch on her shoulder, and she flinched, but he didn't back off. He held on until she raised her eyes to meet his. Then he said, "Look, I'm asking you this stuff because I'm thinking about offering you a place to stay. Room and board in exchange for helping out around here."

There was a long pause while a whole host of expressions played across Nell's face. It took nearly twenty seconds for her to understand what Marlon had said. Her eyes got wide, and she shouted, "What!? Marlon! Are you for real?" She jumped up, bouncing.

"Yeah. It's not the Ritz or anything, but you see that little travel trailer over there? You wouldn't even have to see me if you don't want to. It'd be your own space. You could keep your delivery job in the afternoons for spending money."

Nell was bouncing around the driveway. "Woo-hoo! Oh my God, Marlon! You just sorted my life all the way out!"

"I don't know about that, but maybe it'll give you some breathing space. Help you work out what you want to do."

Marlon was the third great influence on Nell's life.

The Magic Airplane

The child lay on her stomach, elbows supporting her upper body, legs bent at the knees, bare feet in the air. She rested half in, half out of a cardboard box turned on its side. Four holes had been cut into the cardboard to form front and side windows—her Daddy had cut the holes for her before he left for his job flying a big airplane because she wasn't allowed to handle sharp things. Now, five-year-old Amelia worked to fashion an instrument panel using crayons, a glue stick, and a bunch of buttons from a rusty old cookie tin her grandmother had given her to play with.

She heard a voice coming from her grandmother's kitchen as she rubbed out a crooked line with an art-gum eraser. The voice rasped out some indistinct words. Then, so loud it made her jump, there was a *thump* on the table.

"Do you understand me?" the voice barked.

Amelia heard her Grandmother make a tiny sound. She grabbed the black crayon and furiously worked on coloring in the area around the instrument panel of her cockpit. Her Daddy had promised her the airplane would fly and that she would be able to use it any time she liked to fly to him. She needed to get it finished right *now*, so she could go and get her Daddy. It was her only hope.

A man she didn't know had burst in through the kitchen door while Grandma was washing dishes. Amelia, lying on the living room floor, could see him and his gun by looking under the sofa, but he couldn't see her. She'd lain under the sofa for a little while trying to figure out what to do. The bad man made Grandma sit down and used the big roll of silver duct tape from the junk drawer to tape Grandma's ankles to the chair and her hands behind her. Amelia thought about dialing 911, like her teacher taught her at kindergarten, but she didn't have a phone. Amelia had seen the bad man get the cell phone out of Grandma's pocket.

Then she remembered her airplane and set to work as fast as she could. If she could just get it done in time, before the bad man hurt Grandma, she'd be able to fly off and get her Daddy to save them. But she was hurrying too fast, coloring outside the lines. She rubbed furiously at a mistake with her eraser, but she pushed too hard. The packing tape that connected the bottom flap of the box to the sides gave out and she fell through the main control panel, making a loud *kerfwump* noise.

"Who's there?" the bad man shouted.

"It's only my cat," Grandma said. Her voice sounded weak, almost like a whisper.

Amelia didn't have to look to know Grandma was crying. She also knew that Grandma was trying to protect her. They didn't have a cat. She crept over to Grandma's desk where the Scotch tape dispenser sat. Then she tiptoed back to her plane—quiet as a mouse, ducking and darting around the furniture, never taking her eyes off the kitchen door. She slowly, slowly pulled a piece of tape off the roll and pushed it down onto the sharp edge of the tape dispenser to cut it, but she looked away toward the kitchen, and the tape wrapped itself around her finger and stuck together. She almost said a bad word, the one she'd gotten in trouble for the day before, but she remembered in time that she had to be quiet.

A chair moved and a loud slap came from the kitchen. "*What* do you think you're doing, old woman?" the stranger shouted.

Grandma sniffed.

"I asked you a question."

"I was getting a cramp," Grandma said.

"Looked like you were trying to get up out of that chair to me," the man said. "Do it again and I'll do more than slap you."

Amelia started to cry and her hands shook. She couldn't help it, but she knew the bad man would hurt her Grandma again if she didn't get the plane done. She also knew that if she didn't do a good job, the magic wouldn't work, and it wouldn't fly. That's what her daddy had told her, so she took a deep breath and willed her hands to be steady. The man had already started to hurt Grandma, and Amelia had seen bad men on television. She knew it was only a matter of time before he hurt Grandma really badly.

She pulled off another piece of tape, fixing it to one side of the flap with the control panel on it. When she pulled off the next piece of tape, she forgot to be quiet, and the tape dispenser made a *krrrrcht* noise. Amelia froze and watched the kitchen door. It was quiet in the kitchen, and after a minute or so, she raced around to finish the controls. There was just a little more to do, and she was almost done when she felt a big, hot hand close around her ankle.

The man who pulled her out of her airplane was grinning. His teeth were broken and yellow. His breath smelled as sour as vomit.

He said, "Well, looky here. You're a pretty little kitty, aren't you?"

Bracketville, Texas

NOVEMBER 1964

It was the first time I'd gotten to go hunting. Usually, I stayed with one of my grandmothers, but I guess *this* deer lease was kid-friendly because of the beat-up little travel trailer. That's all there was to the place, a travel trailer and a campfire in a pasture of dry grass as tall as me. Scrubby live oak, juniper, and mesquite—tall trees in my four-year-old eyes—edged up to the campsite on two sides and provided homes for white-tailed deer, turkey, and quail. Peggy's husband Nickie owned the land.

I loved the way a twig shoved into the hot embers of the campfire would catch light. That magic occupied hours of my day until Daddy showed me how to clean quail. He pulled off their little heads then made a slit with his pocketknife and pulled the skin off, feathers and all—like when I raised my hands over my head for some grownup to pull my shirt off. Daddy made me try pulling the skin off one of the little dead birds, but I couldn't do it right, so I just watched him do it. I was with Daddy while Mommy and Peggy took a turn hunting. Peggy's husband, Nickie, and her mama were there somewhere too.

Mommy and Peggy sure had a good time hunting that afternoon. They didn't see any deer or quail, probably because

13

they couldn't quit talking, Daddy said, but they did shoot an armadillo. That made them laugh all night. They told the story over and over about Mommy grabbing the armadillo's tail as it ran into a hole. "Bad idea," she said. "Have you ever tried to pull one of those suckers out of its hole? They're strong!" Meanwhile, Peggy shot the poor thing in the butt with a .410.

There was a lot of laughing in the trailer that night. We must have eaten the quail me and Daddy cleaned, but what I remember most is watching Peggy's mama, who was a nurse, pierce Peggy and then Mommy's ears with a giant needle. Trouble was, nobody had any earrings to put in the holes. I don't know why they didn't think of that before they started. They ended up using straw from a broom to keep the holes open till they could get home and buy earrings. Years later, Mommy's earrings still didn't sit quite right.

Mommy tried to get me to go to bed, but I couldn't sleep. They were laughing too much.

Peggy said, "You sure are a good girl. You want some Coca-Cola?" She was pouring fresh drinks.

"Tell Miss Peggy thank you, baby," Mommy said. She lit a cigarette that filled the whole trailer with mentholated smoke. I liked watching it swirl and swoosh out the door when Peggy opened the door to take some drinks outside to the men.

When she came back in, Peggy asked Mommy, "Y'all trying for another one?"

Mommy rolled her eyes my way. "Little pitchers have big ears." I knew they were talking about babies. Mommy sounded like she might cry. I didn't connect the dots then—I was barely four, but she had been in the hospital that summer because my baby sister came too early and died. Mommy took a big sip of her drink. "What about you?" she asked.

Peggy rummaged around in her purse and pulled out a crumpled piece of paper with messy writing on it and slapped it on the table. "I'm through! Looky what I got!"

"Pills? You got 'em already?"

"Not yet."

"What's Nickie say?"

"I haven't told him."

"You haven't *told* him?"

"Why should I? We can practice for a while longer—wait for a good crop to pay the hospital bills."

Mommy got real quiet, then started crying.

Peggy's mama patted her back and handed her a Kleenex.

"Oh, hell. I'm sorry. I didn't even think," Peggy said.

"The doctor told me to quit trying. He offered to tie my tubes, but Bobby wants a boy."

Peggy's mama said, "Why would a doctor say that honey? At your age?"

"Three strikes and you're out, I guess. They come earlier and earlier. Cervical incompetence they call it."

Peggy's mama nodded. "I read about a technique called a purse-string suture."

"Tried that this last time." Mommy took a long drink of her grown-up Coke and lit another cigarette. "I'm lucky to have my good girl right here." She ran her fingers through my hair.

Everybody looked at me, and Peggy's Mama smiled. "You were a preemie too, weren't you, baby?"

Mommy said, "Thank God she was hungry."

In the morning, Mommy and Peggy were still sleeping and Peggy's mama had already gone out, so I got my rubber boots on all by myself and poured my very own milk like a big girl. Then I went outside and gathered sticks to shove into the embers of the campfire. That's what I was doing when Daddy got up. He and Nickie had slept outside on air mattresses. He said, "Hey sugar, where's your mama?"

"Sleeping."

"Let's go wake her up. We got to get packed."

Inside the trailer, Nickie was standing beside the table looking at that piece of paper Peggy showed us. His face was red.

Daddy looked over his shoulder, then hollered for Mommy, "Time to go, Babe."

Nickie just stood there staring at that piece of paper.

Nobody said much while Mommy packed our stuff. Everybody hugged and we got in the Jeep. Peggy's mama walked up to say goodbye and hug Mommy, so we all heard Nickie yell, "What in the *hell*, Peggy?"

Peggy's mama said, "Y'all go on. It's a long way to Houston. I had a good time last night."

Ode to a Delivery Girl

Tammy, the delivery girl from Piggly Wiggly, flicked the kill switch and kicked the stand for the motorbike down. She left her helmet on the seat but kept her driving gloves on as she lifted the groceries out of the carrier attached to the rear fender. She took a steadying breath and looked up the rocky, uneven path to the lighthouse. Even though the guy who lived there always tipped well, he hated to come out here to meet her. Tammy didn't know the man's whole name, just Jud. He always paid in cash, so there wasn't any credit card receipt to clue her in.

The guy had lived alone out at the lighthouse for as far back as Tammy could remember. Ten years, maybe? Mr. Grigsby, Tammy's manager, said Jud was from Canada. Why not? Might as well be from Timbuktu. He wasn't local, that was for sure. Odd. That's what he was.

He never made eye contact, and he never left the light-house. Tammy's mom said he was probably a shut-in—one of those people with agoraphobia or something. She'd read the definition on WebMD from her phone: "It's not unusual to worry sometimes. But when your fears keep you from getting out into the world, and you avoid places because you think you'll feel trapped and not be able to get help, you may have agoraphobia."

It was just getting dark. Seemed like every time she'd ever been out here with groceries, it was getting dark. That's part of what made the trip up to the stupid old lighthouse so hard. You couldn't see where you were going. Then a wave would break over the point and send spray back down the path. The steps were uneven and slick. Tammy was grumbling to herself and trying to pick her way over the rocks when one of those damned waves came out of nowhere and took her feet right out from under her.

"Shit!" she said as the eggs smashed. Jud appeared out of the dark ahead of her as she was dusting her knees and inspecting the damage to her favorite jeans.

"Oh, dear. I'm sorry, young lady." His locks were in wild disarray. His dark, gold-rimmed spectacles looked out of place in the evening gloom. "Come in and let me get you a towel. Did you hurt yourself?"

"I'm okay," Tammy said, but she really wasn't. She didn't notice the blood on her hand until she reached for the grocery bags. She had caught herself with her right hand, and though the driving glove had taken the brunt of it, it had torn to reveal a bleeding gash where a sharp rock had cut through the meat of her palm. "Oh, shit."

"Let me see." The lighthouse keeper turned the girl's hand over and examined the injury. "Good thing you were wearing gloves. It might have been worse." He looked up and met Tammy's eyes over the rims of his glasses.

Tammy had never noticed the strange color of the lighthouse keeper's eyes. Even in the dim light they appeared to shine. Tammy looked away and told herself it was just an illusion because dark skinned people with light colored eyes always looked like that.

Jud pushed his glasses up to the bridge of his nose and cleared his throat. "Come on in. Let me bandage that for you."

Tammy was surprised by the bright interior of the lighthouse.

Jud led her to an upholstered chair beside the fireplace and got her a wad of paper towels. "Put pressure on that," he said.

A few minutes later, Jud returned with a cup of cocoa. Then, sitting in a hardback chair facing her, he reached for her hand with his own hand palm up. He turned the injured hand to the light ever so gently. He said, "Shame your glove is ruined. May I cut it off?"

"It's toast already." She shrugged as she said it, trying to sound tough. Truth was, it hurt. And looking at the blood that continued to pool in the jagged tear made it hurt worse.

Jud said, "This is deep, young lady. What is your name, by the way?"

"Tammy."

"Well, Tammy, I could take care of this for you if you trust me to do it, but I can also call someone to come for you."

"I can drive, but I feel bad your eggs are broken. Probably squashed the bread too."

"I'm not worried about that. We need to get you patched up."

"Just wrap it up with some paper towel. This is my last delivery for the night. Mr. Grigsby will let me off after that. I'd usually stay till closing—stocking shelves and stuff—but this will get me out of that."

Nothing like the logic of a teenager, Jud thought. "I can do a little better than that," he said, as he produced a bottle of hydrogen peroxide and cleaned the wound. Then he placed a thick gauze pad over the still-bleeding gash and wrapped it tight enough that it wouldn't shift while Tammy maneuvered her motorbike. When he was finished, he said, "It's an on-the-job injury. Manager'll see it's looked after, just don't leave it to get infected."

"You sound like a doctor or something."

"Medic in the service. I could sew it up for you, but I don't have any anesthetic."

"Oh." Tammy finished her cocoa with a gulp and said, "Well, thanks for the drink. You don't have to pay if I drop your stuff. Boss will send somebody else out first thing tomorrow with some more."

"Nonsense. I've already written the check."

"I like your place, by the way."

Jud flushed. The compliment, apparently, surprised him, unaccustomed as he must be to having company. "Thank you. Would you like the tour?"

Tammy's interest showed in her eyes, but she decided against the additional delay. "I really need to get back."

"Of course. Maybe next time when there's no danger of you bleeding to death."

Both of them laughed.

The following week, Tammy was prepared. She brought a large canvas backpack to carry the groceries and a flashlight, so she could watch where she was putting her feet.

Jud saw her coming and met her at the door, with a smile like they were old friends. "How's your hand, Tammy?"

Tammy grinned back. "It's getting better. Mr. Grigsby made me get stitches, but the swelling is mostly gone down now. I couldn't drive for a few days, though." She held up her bandaged hand and waved it back and forth. "He sent you some extra eggs and bread to make up for the ones I smashed last time."

"Tell him I said thank you."

Tammy nodded, reluctant to meet the lighthouse keeper's eyes. She couldn't have said why. An awkward silence followed.

Jud finally reached out and said, "May I get my things from your pack?"

"Oh, sure. Sorry." Tammy handed the pack over the threshold.

"Come in for a minute. You can have a look around while I unpack this." He pointed at the staircase and said, "You're welcome to go up."

"Cool, thanks." Tammy walked the outer edge of the round room looking at small things Jud had collected from the beach—a brass spike, some driftwood, sea urchin shells. She came to the kitchen door and peered in to see Jud putting canned goods away. Not part of the tower, it was a rectangular room with a simple wooden table and chairs, a wood stove and an old-fashioned sink built off to the side.

Jud looked up, strange eyes peering over his glasses, "The best view is two flights up. I'll just be a few minutes."

Tammy followed the spiral stairs up to the next floor which was made of wide old wooden planks that must have had a hundred years' worth of varnish on them, they were so shiny. It figured. What else was there for lighthouse keepers to do? There was a narrow bed, a writing desk, and a bookshelf. It was Jud's personal space, and Tammy felt uncomfortable there, so she carried on up the stairs to the third floor.

Four big windows were cut into the thick walls: north, south, east, and west. Tammy could tell the directions because they corresponded with a giant compass rose painted on the floor. A telescope sat beside the south-facing window, and Tammy could see the shape of the Ferris wheel in the derelict carnival grounds across the bay. The silhouetted rides looked strangely beautiful against the darkening sky—just a few streaks of sunset hues behind them.

"They ought to tear that old place down," Jud said.

Tammy jumped. "You scared me!"

"I used to work there."

"At the carnival?"

"When it was still alive. People used to have fun there."

"You were a carnie?"

"Yep. Left Toronto when I was seventeen."

Tammy nodded, not sure what would be polite to ask. Feeling like she really shouldn't be here in this man's home. He was odd, and she ought to feel uncomfortable, but she didn't.

Jud continued. "Seems like another life. It was twenty-four years ago."

"Did you know that crazy old clown, Krinkles?" The murderous clown was an urban legend in the town.

Jud rested his hand on the telescope. "That crazy old bastard still hangs out there." He swung the scope around and fiddled with the focus. "You ever see him?" He looked at Tammy with a straight face.

"Seriously?" Tammy made a crooked, scoffing face. "Nobody has ever seen him that I've heard about."

"I am serious as a heart attack."

"Naw, man. He's just a bedtime story to frighten little kids," she said, but her skin crawled.

"Not really. I knew him. I saw what he did—what he became." Jud's voice had gone soft.

"What he did?"

"It was right before they closed the park. He was there when those kids died. I could never prove it. It was dark, and I wasn't able to tell exactly what he was up to, but he shouldn't have been where he was when those kids fell."

"Whoa! You saw the accident?"

"Tried to help those poor children. There wasn't anything any of us could do for them." Jud shook his head. "I quit after that. The DA closed the park right after. I was lucky to find a job here."

"You don't get lonely out here by yourself?" The words were out of Tammy's mouth before she had time to second guess the etiquette of asking the question.

Jud smiled. "No. I like the quiet. I can keep the light on, warn ships away. It's simple. The stakes are low. As long as I turn the light on, I can't mess it up." Just then an antique-looking radio made a noise. Tammy could hear distant sailors talking to each other, and Jud said, "Sometimes I talk to ships passing by."

"But you never go anywhere, right? I mean, you have everything delivered?"

"It's easier that way," he said.

Tammy nodded toward the telescope. "You ever see anything over there—through your telescope, I mean?"

"Once in a while." He motioned the girl to look through the eyepiece.

Tammy leaned in and immediately recognized the rusty old amusement park. She knew what the old carnival looked like from the road since she had to pass it to get to work every day, but the telescope brought the whole place into sharp focus from an angle that allowed a clear view of its internal layout. "I'm surprised you can see so much, even in the dark."

"Good 'scope."

Tammy straightened up. "Well thank you, sir."

"Call me Jud, please."

"Thank you, Jud. I better get back to work now."

Tammy, who lived on the wrong side of town, had plans. She wanted to see the world, and delivering groceries for Piggly Wiggly didn't look like it would get her there. She left the lighthouse that night with visions of that derelict park swirling around in her head.

Several nights later, Jud sat gazing out that same south-facing window and watched a shadow haul itself over the chain-link fence into the carnival grounds. He trained the telescope on the dark shape and was surprised to see that he recognized the intruder. Her bandaged hand gave her away, that and her other hand in a dark leather driving glove.

"Oh, hell. Get out of there, girl," Jud muttered to himself as he followed Tammy's progress through the park. She was checking locks and snooping in doorways. She had her backpack and flashlight, clearly up to some mischief. Jud's sense of impending doom grew as he watched. He debated calling the police, but what would he tell them? "Someone has broken into the old carnival grounds." That would get Tammy arrested if they cared at all. If Jud told the authorities he was worried Krinkles the Clown might do the girl some harm, they'd probably lock *him* up.

After three-quarters of an hour, Jud's neck felt stiff from bending over the telescope, but Tammy showed no signs of leaving the park. She was taking her time going from ride to ride. Jud couldn't quite make out what she was doing, though. About an hour into the adventure, Jud thought he caught a glimpse of another figure following Tammy at a distance—a figure wearing a clown suit.

"Oh, Shit."

Jud, who hadn't left the lighthouse in fifteen years, launched a dinghy from the point and prayed he could make it across the bay in time. He'd phoned 911 just before running out into the night. He didn't need the binoculars he wore around his neck to tell him that he was too late. When the lights came up on the Ferris Wheel, everyone in town must have been able to see them.

"Oh, Tammy," Jud wailed as he dragged the dinghy ashore and ran to the park.

The Sheriff's Deputy found him shouting at the gate. "Jud? Was it you who called? What the hell?" She'd never seen the man away from his lighthouse.

"It's Tammy! She's in there." He didn't need to say more.

The Deputy had bolt cutters, and as soon as the chain fell off the gate, they ran toward the lights.

Tammy was at the base of the Ferris Wheel, her backpack beside her bulging with scavenged copper wire. What she hadn't known was that the power to this ride was live. When she tried to cut the wires between the motor and the control box, 480 volts had arched across her body.

"I need an ambulance at the old fairgrounds," the deputy spoke into her radio.

Jud threw the main switch to cut the power. "Stupid, stupid girl." He wept as he sank down beside Tammy. Outside the pool of light where he crouched beside the dead delivery girl, a mechanical, clattering, clacking sound caught his attention. "Deputy, shine your light over here," he said. And there, bouncing and clattering in the flashlight's beam was a set of wind-up teeth. They appeared to be laughing.

Nebula

"Bula! . . . Bula! . . . Now where the devil is that stupid girl." The very large woman's motorized scooter hummed from one side of the porch to the other. "Bula!"

A twig of a girl in a thin cotton dress, her hair tangled by the wind, came running around the side of the trailer house. She cradled a basket of eggs in one arm. "I'm coming, MeeMaw. Just had to check in with the chickens. A snake came into their house last night and got two of the little red hen's eggs. They were all aflutter."

"They told you that, did they? Do they speak space alien or what?"

"No, MeeMaw. Just regular old chicken talk," Bula said. Her ability to understand and talk to animals had always set Bula apart from other people. 'Course there was more to it than that. Bula knew things without being told, like what people were thinking, and that had gotten her in trouble when she was a very young child because she thought everybody could see the colorful auras and the mind-pictures she picked up from people and animals. Little toddler Bula— mascot of the dressing room at the topless club with a mat under her Mommy's dressing table—liked to point out all of the carefully hidden boo-boos the ladies in the dressing room tried to conceal. She'd reach out to offer sympathy, and sometimes the ladies would hold her. They always felt better when they set her down to go do their acts. But some ladies shied away from her, not wanting her to expose their secrets. And she knew to hide from the manager. He was scary with his black and red aura. Later, when she'd had to go to Texas after her mother got committed, she'd held herself apart. There was an oppressive air of judgment that permeated the little town where her MeeMaw lived. A hairy eyeball accompanied with a clear message so many of the people in the place broadcast 24/7: "I'm going to Heaven and you're not." She didn't hear the actual thoughts in their heads or anything, it was more like she could tell if what they were saying matched their feelings. If someone, person or animal, was communicating with her, she saw a series of images broadcast in her mind like it was a movie screen. The movie often didn't line up with the words coming out of people's mouths, but animals didn't lie. That's how she knew about the snake and the eggs in the hen house.

A couple of times people at school had come to her with their animal problems. "Something's wrong with my dog. Can you talk to him?" That kind of thing. She'd tried it a time or two, but the things she learned didn't help a lot, especially with the dog that said, "Her daddy beat me." 'Course the whole family had been leaning forward to hear what the strange little girl had to say. Bula hadn't ever been invited back to that house again. By the age of nineteen—now—she was used to not having human friends to talk to. MeeMaw had never been her friend, even though she'd been good enough to take Bula in when her mother got locked up. She gave the girl a roof over her head, but she wasn't kind.

"Where's my breakfast, girl?" The great toad of a woman demanded even as she blocked Bula's path to the kitchen with her motorized chair. It was red with a flared front bumper. Bula thought it made MeeMaw look like a Dalek from *Dr. Who.*

"Whatcha want today, MeeMaw? We have eggs, but we're out of bacon. I can't go to the store till I get paid this evening." She squeezed around behind her grandmother carefully setting her basket of eggs on the counter.

"You're just a regular ray of sunshine, ain't you? How about you fix me some of them biscuits like I like. We got bacon fat enough to make gravy, haven't we?" MeeMaw wheezed when she spoke, though the most physical exertion she ever did was fighting her way over the raised doorstep between the living room and the porch. The scooter liked to stall out right at high center. MeeMaw had to get down and push it across if she was home alone. More than once, Bula had come home from work and found her trapped in the opening of the sliding door because she couldn't go one way or the other, and she couldn't get off the scooter. Bula about wet her pants fighting to hold in the laughter as she shoved the scooter and helped the crotchety old woman down so she could go to the bathroom and change her big girl panties, as she liked to call the jumbo-sized pull-ups she wore.

"I don't have time for all that this morning, MeeMaw. Remember? I have to be at work early. I'm opening up today." It was a big deal because it was the most responsibility Bula's boss had ever given her.

"Well Hell's bells, girl. Are you going to just leave me here to starve?"

"Let me scramble you some eggs right quick. I picked a nice tomato, and I can heat up a pork chop from last night."

"Well, I guess that'll have to do."

The floor of the trailer house creaked as the scooter followed the girl around the kitchen blocking her path repeatedly as she hurried between refrigerator and stovetop cracking three eggs straight into the pan.

"You're going to burn 'em like that," the old woman grumbled—peering up over the countertop.

"MeeMaw, I'm going to be late," Bula said, slinging the eggs onto a plate she placed on her grandmother's lap. She didn't often answer back, but on this day, she said, "What would you rather, MeeMaw, perfect eggs or a paycheck?"

While her MeeMaw wheezed and whirred and muttered, her foul mouth full of dry scrambled eggs, the floor creaked and complained beneath her. Bula raced to the bathroom and yanked her hair into a ponytail, brushed her teeth, and ran over her smelly parts with a washcloth—a PTA bath, her mother used to call it—Bula wasn't ever sure if the "a" stood for assholes or armpits, but as a little girl, the "p" and the "t" had made her giggle because they stood for words she wasn't allowed to say. She clipped on her mother's charm bracelet and squeezed past her grandmother on the way to the living room to fish her shoes out from under the swivel rocker where she'd stashed them out of the way of MeeMaw's scooter.

"Bring home some pie this evening. I believe I could eat some of that lemon meringue or coconut cream."

"I'll see what's left, MeeMaw."

"Turn on my stories before you go. I can't get the TV to settle down and quit that flipping." The Motorola Quasar color console had been top-of-the-line in 1970, but it was on its last legs by now, eighteen-and-a-half years on.

Bula unlocked the kitchen door at the Dairy D-Lite at 7:30 on the dot and nearly forgot to clock in in her rush to get the lights on. The cook didn't show up until 7:45, but Bula already had the grill hot for him. A couple of deaf-as-posts old farmers thought they were being discrete shouting at each other.

"That's Alice Marie's girl," said one.

"She favors her Mama, don't she," the other replied.

The first man took a deep look into his coffee cup and slowly shook his head to convey the regret everyone felt for the way things had gone with Alice Marie. She'd been a ragamuffin of a girl who started smoking dope and ran off to California—come back pregnant talking about space aliens. It was every family's worst fear—what they prayed would never happen to their own daughters.

"Uh, uh, uh," said the first man.

Bula was used to being talked about. In a town this small everybody knew everybody's business, and their hearts were mostly in the right places.

While Delbert, the cook, clattered around as if he was doing something, Bula handed him the green-striped slip from her pad. "Here's their order," she said.

Delbert took the order, avoiding her eyes. He acted scared of her. She knew he'd heard the talk, but when Bula tried to reassure him, he said, "I don't play around with any of that hoodoo mess." As he said it, he rubbed his right hand over a tattoo on his left forearm that looked like a wrought-iron railing from the French Quarter. Bula knew from inside his head that it was a talisman to evoke Papa Legba for protection. She also understood from that quick glimpse that Delbert firmly believed that he had made it home from 'Nam with both arms and legs thanks to Papa Legba's protection.

After she delivered the order to the old men, she said, "Delbert, I'm not a witch. I couldn't do anything to hurt you." She didn't know if that was true, but she knew she would never hurt anybody unless they hurt her first.

The cook said, "I know that stuff's real. My auntie's best friend's stepbrother got messed up by a hoodoo man down in New Orleans. Hexed the dude till his Johnson turned black and fell right off."

Bula busted out laughing. The funniest part was the expression on Delbert's face. He was trying to look serious, but the way he opened his eyes wide and pursed his lips just looked funny to her.

Delbert said, "Folks remember when your mama rocked up pregnant and crazy, talking about how the space aliens were gonna come for you and her one day. Your people never believed her. That's why she went back to California to wait for her spaceman to come."

The sun was full up when the boss came in and went straight to the till. "Mornin' Bula," she called over one shoulder, then "Mornin' Delbert," over the other. There weren't more than half a dozen customers that whole day, and when Bula hung up her apron at six o'clock, the boss handed her a pay packet, and their hands touched a little bit, and Bula knew right then what the woman was going to say. "I'm going to have to let you go, sugar. I'm *real* sorry. We just don't have enough business."

Bula nodded. It took her a minute to swallow the lump in her throat and say, "Thank you for keeping me on this long, Ms. White." In that lightning-fast brush with Mrs. White's hand, Bula picked up the woman's deep worry and sadness at having to close the business. It wasn't her fault the town was drying up.

The Greyhound blew past as she walked home, and Bula smelled freedom in the diesel fumes. It felt like the world shifted just the tiniest little bit on its axis.

You took a left off the old highway to get to MeeMaw's trailer down the dirt road you had to be a local to find, hidden back in the hawthorn thicket like it was. There was half an acre left. MeeMaw'd been selling the land off to their cattle rancher neighbor, a little piece at a time for a long time, since her disability check didn't go far enough to cover the taxes and the utilities anymore.

Bula didn't realize she'd forgotten the pie, forgotten all the groceries, in fact, until she was within spitting distance of the house. She braced herself for the chewing out she was about to get, but MeeMaw wasn't on the porch. The cats that lived under the steps greeted her crying that they hadn't eaten all day and that MeeMaw hadn't been out at all.

The smell hit her when she opened the door—like MeeMaw had dropped a full Depends on the floor and run over it with her scooter. That wasn't unusual. What was unusual was the quiet, that and the lump of bitter condescension that had coalesced in the middle of the living room floor around the fallen scooter.

A bit of the rotten floor had finally given way and the scooter had tipped over, spilling MeeMaw out onto the floor. The coroner said she hadn't been dead long when Bula found her. She might have lain there all day. Bula already knew that. She'd been feeling MeeMaw's spirit leaving the house while she waited for someone to come. She'd had to run to the nearest neighbor up the road and borrow his phone to call 911.

Bula fiddled with her charm bracelet while she waited for the bus. She had a one-way ticket to LA and $687 dollars. She'd cried to leave the chickens and the cats under the porch, but they couldn't go with her, and she couldn't stay.

On the bus, nobody sat beside her until Dallas when a cheerful woman named Nita chattered in her ear all the way to LA. When Nita introduced herself, Bula hesitated. "My name's"—*this is a new start, right?*—"My name's Nebula."

Strings of Solace

Carly squeezed her little car into a metered parking space and got out. She hoped the long walk to the campus would give her a chance to clear her mind and get her nerves under control. She was walking around to get her stuff out of the trunk when her right foot slid out from under her, and she hit the pavement. Hard. She pushed herself up and dusted her butt off as she looked around to make sure no one had seen her fall.

Bad omen, she thought. Her left wrist hurt. *Great. Who ever heard of ice on the ground in October, anyway? What must it be like in the winter here?* But there was no use whining about the weather now. She needed to focus on her audition. It was important to Tim that she stick with her goal of getting a degree in music since she'd given that up to move to Chicago and be with him.

Tim Hunt had roared into Taos on his big motorcycle and swept her off her feet. She'd only known him three months when she agreed to marry him, but so what? It felt like a fairy tale. He was her knight on his silver steed, and she was his desperate damsel looking for any escape from her evil stepfather. She'd get used to Chicago—lots of people lived here happily, weather and all.

Carly wrestled the guitar case out of the car and slung her music bag over her shoulder. The voice in her head saying, *this doesn't feel right* was familiar. She'd been ignoring it since she left home with Tim. It sounded like her stepfather.

Focus, she thought, mentally pulling up the audition piece she'd prepared and running through it as she walked. She'd played it a thousand times, knew it backward and forward, but she also knew how quickly she could screw it up.

Her Daddy's smile flashed like sunshine in her memory and brought a lump to her throat. *If Daddy was here*, she thought, *there'd be no problem. I wouldn't be a nervous wreck.* She'd never had stage fright when he was alive, but the music business had eaten her Daddy up. She was twelve when they'd found him dead on the tour bus with his name emblazoned on the side. Music had been a game she played with her Daddy, making up silly songs and setting them to music. Now, when no one else was around, she played just for him. His laughter and beautiful smile kept her going. Playing for other people was the problem.

Carly blamed her stepfather, Billy, for planting the fear of performing in her. He had worked hard to make her stop playing entirely. To him, all musicians were good-for-nothing druggies and alcoholics. Carly couldn't remember a single dinnertime conversation since he'd come into her life that hadn't ended with him yelling something about how she needed to grow up and be responsible—think of an *honest* way to make a living—something that didn't involve music. "You can work the keys on a computer just as well as the keys on a piano," he said.

"I don't even play piano, Billy," Carly would sneer and bolt out of the dining room slamming her bedroom door for emphasis.

Billy, who always had to have the last word, would shout, "I'm not paying for you to study music. You better think up a degree plan that'll get you a real job." So, Carly worked two jobs to pay her own college tuition. She still lived at home, though, so the arguments continued. Her heart hurt from

Billy's constant criticism. His CPA brain couldn't understand that Carly needed music in her life to thrive—to harmonize with that ache in her chest. It was a yearning she couldn't express any other way—an itch she could only scratch by making music.

Her daddy knew what that felt like. He'd defined it for her when he started teaching her to play guitar and sing. They'd spend ages just fooling around with a single minor chord—humming the different harmonies in it. Daddy said, "If it feels like the sound could make you cry, you're in the magic spot." He loved music and sharing it with her. It wasn't his fault about the drugs. She refused to believe that he chose to leave her. Once he started making big money, though, the record company didn't give him any choice. He was on tour way more than he was home. All he did was sleep the last time Carly had seen him. He'd begged off their guitar time saying, "Baby, I need to recharge my batteries. Can we go get some ice cream instead?"

Carly couldn't care less about fame. And she guessed that was the part her asshole stepdad couldn't get. Why would she want the lifestyle that had killed her father? Still, she wanted music in her life. Every day. Her loftiest goal was to become a session musician at a recording studio where she never had to see the audience. Chicago was a great place for that with several big recording studios. She just had to perfect her playing. No, it wasn't even really her playing. She could play, but nobody knew it because of the stage fright. Okay, sure, to be a session musician she'd have to be able to sight-read anything and play several instruments. That's why she needed a music degree. Her Daddy had never learned to read music. He'd been one of those naturals who played so well by ear that he never needed to. He was the front man—a star from the first time he played for anybody. Carly didn't need that. She'd be happy as a nameless backup musician.

She'd tried to explain it to Billy, but he refused to believe there was any good in playing music at all, and Carly's mom agreed. She'd divorced Carly's dad right after his first record hit the charts. Too many groupies, she said. Carly had been little then, and music had been all but banned in their house, so she kept her guitar hidden under the bed—especially when Billy was home, so when Tim roared into her life, and he actually *wanted* her to be a musician, Carly had been so flattered she never thought past the honeymoon. At first she was ashamed that she couldn't play for him, but she was grateful for his encouragement. As a painter who hated to show his work, he recognized her social anxiety.

* * *

She stopped to adjust the bag on her shoulder and get a grip on her thoughts. *Wrong time to drag all that crap up. I'm doing this my way, and Billy can go to hell.*

* * *

The words "School of Music" over a set of double doors announced that she'd found the right building. Hot air hit her with a blast. She searched the directory for Dr. Bonham's office, and her hair crackled as she pulled her stocking cap off. She scraped the hair into a messy ponytail in the elevator. It wasn't the composed look she wanted, but it would have to do. She found the door she wanted. Slipping her coat off, she noticed that her knee was bleeding from her tumble beside the car. *Great.* It stung when she touched it. She tugged on her skirt hoping to hide the scrape, then straightened up and knocked on the door.

"Come."

"Dr. Bonham?" She stopped just inside. "I'm Carly Hunt. I had a ten o'clock appointment?" Her stomach knotted.

"Come in, come in." The tall man acted like he was in a hurry and brushed at invisible lint on his dark suit. "Sit down."

He took her guitar case and set it aside, waved at a chair, then perched on the corner of the desk, his long leg and shiny black shoe dangling uncomfortably close to her. Carly had to tilt her head to look up at him. His cologne was overpowering, and she scooched the chair back as far as she could, then she took in her surroundings. The office felt like a church with wine-dark carpet, oiled-wood paneling, and arched windows. This was a very different sort of music school to the one she'd known in New Mexico, where her professors had worn boots and jeans. Nobody there bothered with cologne. It was too hot for that. There, a happy musical chaos floated in the hallways overlaid with the scent of stale saliva from brass players' spit traps. This place was silent and smelled of furniture polish once you got past the cologne.

"Now, Miss Hunt, why have you come to see me?"

Carly snapped out of her reverie. "I'd like to finish my degree here. I've spent three years at the Taos School of Music, so technically I'm a junior, but I understand it may take me an extra year because I'm transferring." She hesitated, then added, "And it's *Mrs.* Hunt." She looked down at her hands. Her new name felt strange on her tongue.

"We don't accept many transfer students, but I see your transcripts are in order." He placed a pair of reading glasses on his nose and tapped at the papers. "You've done the requisite theory classes. What sort of music have you been playing?" He tilted his head down to look over the tops of the glasses at her.

"Classical mostly . . . a little jazz. My guitar solo work was Sor, Carcassi, Bach . . . some jazz standards . . . voice . . . I did some arranging for the jazz choir, too." It was a confession dragged out in fits and starts.

Dr. Bonham loomed, immaculate and odoriferous glaring down his long nose at her. "Okay," he said. "Play something for me."

Butterflies fluttered in her stomach and her fingers trembled as she took her guitar out of the case and tuned it.

Bonham said, "How about a scale? G Major?"

Whew, she thought, *I can do that in my sleep.*

"The Segovia pattern." He nodded. "Good. Now D minor."

She played that too—even adding a little flourish at the end.

"Alright. Now what piece will you play for me?"

She pushed up straighter in the chair. The professor's proximity made her extra uncomfortable. *Focus*, she told herself. "Sor's A minor etude." She said, handing him a copy of the music she'd memorized.

He gave the page a cursory glance and nodded for her to begin.

She took a deep breath, held it a second, then started to play. *Easy*, she coached herself. She'd started off too fast, but she made it through the first eight bars. *Did I play the dynamics?* She almost fumbled at the twelfth bar out of habit but got through it with only the tiniest of fumbles no one who didn't know the piece would notice. Then she was through the hard bit at the end somehow, magically. Her hands were damp and tingling, but her face flushed in relief when it was over.

Dr. Bonham looked at his watch. "Right, *Mrs.* Hunt," he sniffed. "You know the basics. *If* we can find a slot for you, I'd recommend you play an actual concert piece, if you have one, for the committee." He strolled around the desk to look at his diary. "We don't have room for many students who specialize in *guitar* performance. It's more of a sideline here. Perhaps if you played a second instrument . . . have you sung any opera?"

Carly nodded. "I have. Soprano." She hated squawking around in her upper register, but she had one piece by Francesco Durante memorized in Italian. "I'd need an accompanist."

"Of course. The next step, if the Dean agrees, will be a juried audition with three professors. Keep practicing. We'll be in touch."

* * *

Why on earth did I think I wanted to transfer here? Carly asked herself on the way back to the car. Because Billy, a Chicago native, thought it was a good school? "A degree from there is worth a lot," he'd said, "even in music." She wouldn't be called back. *I wouldn't go to that school if you paid me.* Her gait was slow, and her ears burned with shame. She felt like something Dr. Bonham had scraped off the bottom of his shiny-fucking-shoe.

As she came within sight of her car, she thought, *it is a charming area.* Shop windows and cafés beckoned. *Oh, well, guess I'll never get to know you.*

She passed a music store with antique instruments in the window and went halfway down the block before turning back. *Why not? I've got nowhere to be.* The shop was warm, and the old floorboards creaked. The door blew shut with a bang behind her, and a bell rang above her head. The shelves were crowded and dusty, and a man with a gray ponytail and a bushy beard greeted her from behind a counter to her left. She nodded, pointing to a rack of sheet music. Sometime later, she found a book of Irish jigs and reels, but when she went to pay for it, the shopkeeper was in the back room. She rang the bell by the register. While she waited, she heard a heartbreaking mandolin melody in a minor key, and looking down into the glass case, she saw an old mandolin on display. It had a rounded back like a lute. When the shopkeeper came out, she asked to see it.

"It doesn't play," he said. "We just keep it here for looks. Hasn't been tuned in forever."

"Would you sell it?" she asked. Tim would have a fit that she'd spent money on another instrument she wouldn't play for him, but she felt a wild hair cropping up.

"I suppose. I couldn't ask much—the condition it's in. It's not rare or anything. These little Washburn mandos were pretty popular around nineteen hundred or so. I'd take ninety-five dollars for it."

Surprised at the low price, she said, "Done." Feeling like she'd stolen the little instrument, she made to hurry out of the shop before the man realized his mistake, but she turned back at the door and asked, "What tune were you playing just now?"

"Hmmm?" The man looked up, confused. "When?"

"I mean when you were in the back room."

"Wasn't me, love."

Carly walked back to her car, confused. She'd clearly heard a mandolin playing, but she *was* pleased with her new instrument. On the drive home, she could have sworn she heard the mandolin tune again.

* * *

"I don't know what to do now, Tim," Carly said over dinner that evening.

"Go visit some other schools," he said.

"I'd rather get a job first."

"Knock yourself out." Tim sounded unhappy.

"What's wrong with me working?"

"Did I say anything?"

"No. It was your tone of voice."

"Whatever, Baby, but I thought you wanted to go back to school, finish your degree."

"What's the hurry?" Carly couldn't figure out why Tim was so determined that she stay in school. She resisted on general principle. "I'm not ready to start the application process all over again."

Tim took a sudden keen interest in a story on his iPad, effectively shutting the conversation down.

Carly said, "I hope you don't mind. I bought a mandolin."

"A mandolin?" Tim looked up. "Do you even play the mandolin?"

"Well, no, but it's really pretty. Think of it as art—an antique. I'll have to have it worked on if I ever want to play it."

Tim sighed and said, "Let's see it then."

She got the mandolin, and he turned it over in his paint-spattered hands.

"It'll look nice hanging on the wall if nothing else."

She knew he'd appreciate the visual aesthetic of the instrument even if it didn't actually play anymore. "You're not allowed to paint it."

"Would I do that?" Tim looked innocent. Their apartment was filled with things he'd felt compelled to paint—bright electric-colored dressers and airbrushed lampshades. The downstairs neighbor constantly complained about the noise of Tim's air compressor, so he was looking for a studio space somewhere else. Carly wasn't happy about *that*, but she couldn't stop him.

* * *

Within weeks, Carly was manning the office of a real estate developer who was never there. No one called or came in, and she was bored to tears, but it was a job. With nothing else to do, she searched the Internet for someone to repair her mandolin. She called the Downtown School of Folk Music and made an appointment with their mandolin teacher for the following evening after work.

There were two ancient leather chairs in the big, echoing hall where she sat waiting for Mr. Hansen to arrive. The floors were tiled in a checkerboard pattern that had been bold and new in 1960. The room was heated, but only just. Dan Hansen was middle-aged with a beak of a nose and no hair on top. His hand was warm, and his smile radiated welcome.

"Nice to meet you. I'm Dan."

"Nice to meet you. I appreciate you looking at my mandolin." She handed the instrument to him.

"It's a 'tater bug.' That's what the bluegrass boys call these."

He fished a pick out of his pocket and tuned the instrument by ear. He ran a few scales up and down the little neck with hands that seemed too big to be so precise and quick. Then he tried some chords. The higher he went up the neck the more out of tune it sounded. Dan held the base of the little instrument up to his nose and took a sight down its neck.

"Well, the neck is definitely bowed—you might be able to get a fret job and straighten it out enough to play it."

He gave Carly the number of a luthier he knew. Then he told her classes were starting up the next week. When all was said and done, Carly had agreed to three months of mandolin lessons, and she felt happier than she had in a long time.

She was disappointed to find Tim wasn't home when she got there. She'd wanted to celebrate with him. She poured herself a glass of wine and watched Netflix.

* * *

The next week, Carly had her first lesson. Dan had loaned her a mandolin to use while hers was being repaired. The tiny frets took some getting used to—they were so much closer together than on a guitar. Even so, Dan was impressed that she read music, and he sent her home with exercises and a songbook.

Dan was well known around Chicago for his lightning-fast picking, so Tim and Carly went to a local club one Friday night to hear him play. Dan's band played the blues, and Dan not only made his mandolin do things she had never heard before, he also sang like B.B. King. He was a natural on stage, like her Daddy had been, and Carly found a new measure of respect for her teacher. She was excited on the way home. "I thought Dan was really good. Didn't you?" she said to Tim.

"Uh-huh." He flipped through messages on his phone.

"No, seriously. I didn't expect him to be such a showman. Guess you can't judge a book by its cover."

"He wasn't all that," Tim said.

"But you love blues bands."

"They were fine," Tim said, a little too sharply. "Can we drop it?"

* * *

Six weeks into the mandolin lessons, Dan announced it was time to start rehearsing for the end-of-term concert. His students were to play a short six-song set, then lots of other groups would play as well. Rehearsals were set for Saturday afternoons.

On the first Saturday, Carly had her guitar and her mandolin packed up and ready to go and she was putting on her coat when Tim looked up from his sketch pad and said, "Where are you going?"

"Rehearsal, don't you remember? Saturdays for the next six weeks till the concert."

"No, I don't remember anything about that."

"It's not a problem, is it?"

"Maybe. What am I supposed to do? I thought Saturday was our day to spend together."

"I'll be gone a couple of hours, tops. I'll pick up something nice for dinner on the way home."

"Who else is going to be there?"

"I don't know. Dan—some other students. I haven't met them yet." She set the guitar case down and put her hand on her hip. In a voice that sounded sharper than she'd intended, she said, "What do you think we're gonna be doing? Having an orgy?"

Tim slapped his sketchpad down on the table and stood up. "Don't bother with dinner. I'll get a pizza at the studio."

"What?" Carly snapped. "Oh, that's fine. You go to the studio." She got louder as she went along. "I like spending my nights alone." She was spitting with the force of the last few words, but Tim didn't hear. He was halfway down the back stairs.

* * *

Carly offered a close-lipped smile as Dan introduced her around to the rest of the musicians. She was the only girl in the group. There was a stand-up bass, two banjos, a guitar, a fiddle, and a mandolin, in addition to Carly's mandolin and guitar. The rehearsal was more of a brainstorming session to work out their set list, and when it was done, Carly had no recollection of anybody's name or what she was supposed to practice.

Dan stopped her on the way out. "Carly, is something wrong?"

"Not really. Fight with my husband."

"I know how that goes. I was married once. Want to talk about it?"

"No. Yes. I don't know. I mean he's being so unreasonable! He's actually jealous of me rehearsing," Carly said.

"I've heard that one before. It's pretty common among musicians."

"Yeah. My mom and dad divorced over him being away on tour."

"Your dad's a musician?"

"Was. He's dead now."

"I'm sorry to hear that. What did he play?"

"Guitar."

"Anybody I'd know?"

"I'm embarrassed to say."

"Embarrassed?"

"My dad was Max Santiago."

"*The* Max Santiago? From the Santiago Band?"

Carly nodded.

"Wow! I had no idea!"

"Yeah. I don't share that very often."

Dan said, "I've got a gig to get to or I'd buy you a beer. Go home. Work it out. He'll come around."

* * *

Carly took the El train home. It took her past Tim's studio, so she stopped. The building was run down, but it had big west-facing windows that caught the evening light. She rang the buzzer at street level. No answer. She tried two more times, then called his cell. Nothing. *He must have gone home*, she thought, but when she got home, he wasn't there either.

When she heard him coming in after midnight, she met him in the kitchen.

"Where have you been?" she asked.

"At the studio."

"Really? You weren't there when I came by," she said.

"You came to the studio?"

"Yes, I did. Six o'clock. I thought maybe we could make up and have a nice evening."

"I must have gone out to dinner."

"That would be why you didn't answer your phone either, I suppose."

"I left it in the studio."

"Whatever." Carly marched down the hallway and closed the bedroom door in his face.

* * *

Over the next few weeks, Carly saw Tim less and less. He started going straight to the studio after work in the evenings and staying there all night.

The Saturday rehearsals went alright, and since Carly was the new kid, they suggested that she mostly play rhythm guitar where she felt most comfortable with only one short solo on a mandolin piece. That suited Carly just fine, and everyone was pleased when she volunteered to sing harmony. Adding a woman's voice to the mix enhanced their overall sound tremendously. They asked her to sing lead on one tune and scrambled to find just the right piece settling on

"Wayfaring Stranger." She agreed because the guys insisted. Besides, it was a song she already knew, so she figured she wasn't likely to mess it up, though she was terrified of singing lead. She stumbled through it the first time they ran it, and she told Dan in her lesson the next week that she didn't know if she could sing the song, but he brushed it off saying, "Who you afraid of? It's just going to be a bunch of other music students."

* * *

The day of the concert, Carly was a nervous wreck. She went through the motions of getting ready, putting on deodorant twice just to be sure. Tim was in the apartment for a change, and underfoot all morning. Still, she was glad of the company and told him, "I feel like I'm gonna throw up. Can you imagine if I hurled right there on the stage?"

"I think it would be funny, but you're not going to do that."

"Tim, I don't just want to get through it. I want to do a good job, support the group."

"Why, Baby? It's just a bunch of students. Once this show is over you can quit this nonsense and find a real music school."

"Nonsense? You think this is nonsense?" She slammed her mascara tube down on the counter and wheeled on him. "I can't understand what you want, Tim. Go to a fancy school, don't work. What are you thinking? Do you also want me to be barefooted and pregnant? Teaching the children in the living room? Dinner on the table at all hours of the night whenever you decide to come home?"

"I didn't say that, Baby. Calm down."

"Screw you, Tim. I've got this. Thanks for the motivation. I wouldn't want to interrupt whatever you get up to when you're," she made air quotes, "painting."

"What's that supposed to mean?"

"You know what it means, Tim. King of the double standard. Who you doin', darlin'? Cause it damn sure isn't me."

Carly was shaking with rage instead of nerves now. She hadn't planned to have this conversation, but it was too late to take the words back, so she kept going. "Fuck off and die, Tim. Take your things and leave. I want a divorce. I never want to see you again."

The words surprised Carly as much as they did Tim. Up to that point, she hadn't even dared to think them, but for the first time in a long time, she got a tingling sensation along the backs of her arms that told her she was heading in the right direction. She searched herself for feelings about Tim. There were none.

Tim raised his hand as if to slap her, but Carly didn't back down. Her eyes blazed, and Tim backed away, grabbed his coat, and left.

*　*　*

The hall was packed. The Downtown School of Folk Music occupied an old high school building with a big auditorium, and the old wooden theater seats creaked and rattled as people shuffled through the rows to sit with their friends. Carly hadn't been in the auditorium before, and the sound of the crowd brought a fresh crop of butterflies to life in her belly. She was nearly hyperventilating when the bass player tapped her on the shoulder and pointed to the stage to indicate that it was time to go on.

For the first song, Carly strummed her guitar at the back of the group. She may have hit a few wrong chords, but nobody noticed. Then the banjo and mandolin player in front of her stepped away from each other, and Carly was supposed to step forward and take the microphone. She felt like she would pass out in the dazzling lights. Beads of sweat ran down from her armpits. She imagined her blouse was stained with it. She did her deer-in-the-headlights impression for what seemed like ten minutes. Then Dan walked out and took the mic to welcome the audience and introduce the band.

"Good evening everyone. Thank you for coming out to hear this term's budding bluegrass musicians. They have all worked hard rehearsing this program for you. Tonight, you will see some familiar faces up here, along with a couple of promising newbies." He named the boys in the band and finished with, "and Carly Hunt on rhythm guitar, mandolin, and vocals."

He reached over and squeezed her shoulder as he said her name, then he turned to her expectantly.

What was he waiting for? She couldn't remember what came next.

"Guitar," he mouthed.

Oh, that's right, he was supposed to trade her guitar for her mandolin. That was it. Carly ducked her head and closed her eyes as she lifted the guitar strap over her head. What song was she supposed to sing again? How did it start? *God help me remember the words.*

Dan took the guitar and held out her little tater bug mandolin. He lifted the strap over her head, and whispered in her ear, "Sing pretty. The boys are right here to help you out."

As her hands touched the mandolin it hummed like it couldn't wait to play, and Carly thought of her Daddy's smile. Her eyes filled with tears, and her voice broke as she started to sing around a big ol' lump in her throat, but that only made the music sweeter. "I am a poor wayfaring stranger, traveling through this world of woe." The sound of the boys behind her lifted her and held her safe through the song, and the little mandolin felt like it played itself.

When the song was over, the audience was quiet for a second, then she heard Dan hoot and people started standing up. She turned around and the boys were all clapping too. Dan walked over and called her name out loud and slipped her a handkerchief. She blew her nose and finished the set.

Nell—On Being Prepared

It was time to take inventory, make sure she had everything she needed. Hard times were coming. Siege—at least that's what she feared. Her mother brought her up in the Reagan era, shopping at Sam's Club, buying mayonnaise by the case, toilet paper by the pallet, giant containers of garlic salt and dried parsley, tube socks by the dozen, and enough coffee bricks to build a skyscraper. Nell was more pragmatic than that, and it was just her and Bug she had to worry about. She knew when the big bad times came, she'd only be able to feed Bug so long, so she'd always let him run down a rabbit or a squirrel. And she had fishing tackle and a sturdy rod—plenty good enough for the bass and catfish she came across.

Bug, a Rottweiler-sized creature with an odd, mottled coat, could take care of himself. With his amber eyes and his ability to blend into shadows, he was more demon than dog to look at. He knew how to act in public, did exactly what Nell told him in whispered-under-her-breath commands and hand signals, but she only ever had room for a couple of cases of canned meat. Kibble wasn't going to cut it. It'd be cruel to allow that to take up space better used to contain compact foods like dried rice and beans that would sustain them longer, so she and Bug ate from the one pot of rice and beans with the occasional meat on the side. When she was in a town, she'd buy fresh fruit and veg, otherwise, she foraged mushrooms, wild herbs, berries, and nuts.

Nell made a note in a manky-looking spiral notebook, "corned beef hash, bouillon cubes," and she flipped to the next page where a penciled heading read, "Guns and Ammo." There had not been a day since her Daddy had given her her first gun, a single-shot .410 shotgun, when she was six years old that Nell had not been armed. Her daddy had had six inches sawed off the stock, so it fit her. He taught her to shoot it, clean it, and take care of it. And she'd always kept a gun, in preparation for when the shit hit the fan. Daddy had evaporated when she was ten. But her mama had kept the long guns in her bedroom closet and a little pistol in the nightstand, though she never needed them. Nell still had the .20-gauge shotgun, the .22 rifle, and a little Smith and Wesson .38 Special. She didn't use them, but they were there just in case, and she kept them clean. Fired them occasionally out in the middle of nowhere, testing that her aim was still true, and the ammo was still viable.

In her parents' day, it was the Russians and nuclear war, they were waiting for. Now? Nell was ready for any-damned-thing. She tried to keep her opinions to herself when she got among people, tried not to side with anybody, because there was so much nonsense in the air you couldn't quite tell who to trust. Some crazy, twisted logic in the 7-11 could get you killed. And on top of that, it looked like there might be another world war, gangs were running wild, cops were killing civilians, banks were failing. If this wasn't Tribulations, Nell wasn't sure what was.

She had been laying in supplies all her life in a never-ending cycle. Seemed like she just settled in and got things the way she liked them when it was time to pick up sticks and move, at which point the process would start all over. She traveled in different vehicles, mostly derelict. Wheezing rattle-trap pickups and vans made their final journeys with Nell. She'd leave them where they quit and go with a whispered wish that the provisions she left behind would serve someone else who needed them. And her "go gear" was all strapped to a backpacker's frame. It weighed sixty-two pounds fully loaded, and Bug had saddle bags to carry some cans if they had to walk.

Nell traded on her mechanics' skills, spending a season here and a season there, living rough unless she came across an unoccupied cabin or some good Samaritan rocked up and offered to pay her rent for a while. Most garages had a space in a storage building she could use for a few weeks. She'd gotten good at fortifying a space quickly, but it took constant vigilance, keeping the rice bag full, and coffee enough for the morning. She would really miss coffee, and she hated to run out of salt. She could eat all manner of crap, but it needed to be seasoned.

She lowered her double-layered masks, pulled a single baby wipe from a box by the door of the shed—that's all it was, a garden shed—and wiped the day's grime off her face. She could feel the tension in the air. It was time to pack up, load the old Jeep Cherokee she'd been working on, give Bug the last of the kibble. It wasn't clear yet which way she needed to head, but she'd be ready.

Wrong Way River

William Hardy held his smartphone to his right ear while mashing his left hand over his other ear, straining to hear the voice crackling through the static.

"I must have taken a wrong turn after the river, Daddy. The pavement stopped a while back and there's nowhere to turn around."

"Hold on, honey, I'm trying to find it on the map."

Will's only child, Melissa, was driving up to join him for a week of rest and relaxation in scenic West Virginia. An old army buddy had lent them the cabin, and it was the first time there for both of them. They were looking forward to hiking and bird watching while they caught up on everything that had gone on for both of them since the last time they'd met.

"What? You're breaking up, Dad."

"According to my map," Will shouted into the phone. He'd stepped out onto the porch in the hope that the reception would be better outside, "you shouldn't be anywhere near the river. I can't even see any roads in that area."

"*Say goodbye,*" rasped a strangely accented voice.

"Can you hear another voice on the line, Melissa?"

"What? There's too much static."

"*Sad to say . . .*" came a sibilant hiss.

"Melissa? Is that you? Did you hear that voice?"

"Dad? Can you hear me? You're breaking up."

"She's mine now."

"That voice, Melissa . . . Melissa?"

The line was dead.

Will paced as he waited, expecting Melissa to round the bend in the drive and crunch over the pine needles leading to the cabin any minute. He had been laying a fire in the fireplace when his cell phone vibrated across the table, signaling her call. As the sun set, the air chilled, and he returned to light the fire and let it do its work.

He'd arrived at noon and spent the day unpacking and reveling in the crisp autumn weather. The mountains were ablaze with color. He had planned this week as a time for them to reconnect. They'd remained close following the divorce, but they didn't get to spend much time together since Melissa had gone to college out of state. A week in the woods promised to be just what they needed.

When Melissa didn't arrive after an hour and a half, Will dialed 911. As the crow flies, the cabin wasn't far from the gas station–general store that passed for a town on the map, and he'd have called there first, but he didn't have a number for that place, couldn't even recall the name of it. As it turned out, that's where the 911 call landed in any case. The Sheriff received the call right away, but the land rose steeply around a deep gorge, and the roads snaked and switched back multiplying the distance by road. It took the sheriff nearly two hours to reach the cabin.

When he finally got there, Will could tell the weather-beaten man, brimmed hat in hand, was no stranger to sharing grief. Sheriff Hamilton had spoken to other distraught family members after someone they cared about had gone missing or been in an accident. He knew the "right" things to say. It was something in the way he looked away, allowing his voice to catch when he spoke. There was a weight and sorrow to the man that carried a deeper understanding.

The region had a reputation for odd disappearances, but Will didn't know that, and the Sheriff didn't mention it. Instead, he sized Will up, and seeing the military bearing of the man, he led with a simple question. "Tell me what you know, Mr. Hardy."

"Sheriff," Will replied, his voice calm, his face hard, but his eyes wild, "my daughter should have been here three and a half hours ago. I was talking to her on the phone when the line went dead. We were trying to work out where she'd made a wrong turn. I'm worried she's lost or out of gas out there in the cold. She's a smart girl, knows to stay with the car, but you just never know." Will's imagination had already shown him dozens of potential disaster scenarios from terrible crashes where she'd gone over a ledge to compound nightmares where a bear had found her. He didn't mention any of those fears. Instead, he directed the Sheriff to the map he'd been using while he was talking to Melissa.

Will's direct, matter-of-fact approach told the Sheriff enough about what sort of man he was dealing with—an outdoorsman, rather than a hysterical tourist. Seeing Will's need to do something, he focused on the practical and produced an aerial survey map which he compared to the tourist map Will had marked with a permanent marker to show Melissa's route to the point where she'd turned off the main road as best he could figure.

"Mister Hardy, I been living here all my life, and there just isn't a road anywhere around there. No river either. I know you want to go look for her right now, but we can't do much until daylight. I'll put out an alert and let the local park ranger know to be on the lookout. She's . . . odd, but she knows these woods better than anybody. I'll also have my deputy drive out to the location you marked on this map and see if she can see any evidence of trouble on the road. That's really all we can do tonight."

"I'd like to ride along with the deputy."

The sheriff raised his hand and shook his head. "It's best if you stay put in case Melissa turns up or calls. We'll let you know if we find anything at all, but if she hasn't turned up by morning, this right here is where we'll start looking." He pointed to an X on the topographical map. "We'll muster at this turn-out at six a.m. Wear hiking boots and bring climbing gear if you have it. I'm sorry we can't start hunting for her sooner."

Will's heart sank. He couldn't bear the thought of his little girl having to spend the night alone in the woods on some moonshiner's secret road, but he tried his best to be positive. "She's bound to find her way to a main road by then. I hate that you had to come way out here, Sheriff." Will set his phone to charge so he wouldn't miss a call for lack of battery and walked the plank floors until he finally sank into a hardbacked rocker and slept dreaming fitfully of bears and psychopaths circling around his daughter's car.

At six a.m., he met up with the sheriff, a deputy, and a park ranger along with half a dozen civilians with horses and dogs. Several pick-up trucks and a horse trailer sat at precarious looking angles—left wheels on the solid line outlining the road and the right wheels much lower, in the deep pine litter beside the winding road. Will had to park several hundred yards from the place where the people were assembled, and it tried his patience that he couldn't just drive into the big middle of the gathering and stop. But he ground his teeth and practiced deep breathing.

The atmosphere among the assembled searchers was almost like a celebration. These people all knew each other, and they talked and laughed together amiably, like it was just another run-of-the-mill search. At the far side of the clearing, a short woman in sheriff's khakis appeared to be arguing with a taller woman in a green uniform and a bright orange scarf.

The sheriff saw Will coming and intercepted him. "Mr. Hardy, this way. Let me introduce you to Ranger Angie Wolfe, your search partner."

The woman in the forest green uniform turned to greet him. Her thick, dark hair was tied in a bright, road-crew orange scarf, and she wore heavy eye makeup. "Mister Hardy," she said and extended her hand as she locked eyes with him and stared hard enough to bore a hole through his head.

The Sheriff interrupted the strange woman's gaze, saying, "Deputy Lopez and I will be taking turns on the search since one of us has to be on call at all times."

The shorter woman, Deputy Lopez nodded at Will and put her hat on her head. "See you at lunch, Sheriff." With that she turned and walked away.

Teams formed and radio protocol was explained, though it seemed everyone there apart from Will already knew the drill.

Two hours later, when Will and Ranger Wolfe, who had been combing through underbrush looking for clues, stopped for water, Will asked, "How often do you people have to do this?"

"Do what, Mister Hardy?"

"Search for missing people."

"Sometimes two, three times a year."

"And do you usually find the missing person?"

Wolfe shrugged. "Sometimes." She took a deep breath. "Mister Hardy. You need to be prepared. I don't believe your daughter is in these woods any longer."

Will stopped and stood up straight. He said, "Oh. And you can say that because?"

"If she was here, I would know it." Her resigned voice and her sad eyes made Will's stomach knot up. He didn't try to argue with the illogic of the woman, because he felt it too.

After the lunch break, when no one had found even the slightest trace, Sheriff Hamilton took Will aside. "I hope you don't mind me saying it, but Mr. Hardy, you look like hell. Go back to your cabin. Get yourself a stiff drink. Try to take a nap. I'll let you know if we turn up anything."

The search crew combed the area in ever expanding circles for four days, their numbers dwindling a little each shift as they returned one by one to their regular schedules, but it was rough terrain. At the end of the fourth day, when nobody had seen any indication that Melissa Hardy had ever been there, the Sheriff had to break it to Will that they couldn't afford to continue the search. "If there had been even the slightest trace, we might be able to pull some state funds, Mr. Hardy, but we've got nothing. I'm sorry."

Will's life as he'd known it ended with that last broken cell-phone conversation with Melissa. He never considered returning to work. It took exactly one call to hand his projects off to his business partner in the architecture firm in Pittsburg and arrange to have a little money transferred to his account for groceries and gas each week. His buddy who owned the cabin never really used it, so he didn't mind letting Will stay on there as long as he needed to.

Will spent most days exploring the deepest, darkest woods looking for any sign his daughter had passed that way. He scouted every dirt road and deer track and blazed new trails through thick undergrowth. After a month, though, he knew she must be dead, but even then he was driven to find out what had happened to her. He carried a small backpack and a bed roll and sometimes slept so far from human habitation he imagined he was the only person ever to stop there. In his dreams, Melissa spoke to him, whispering, *"I'll see you at the River. Follow the path to the River."*

A chilly mist filled the glade where Will woke up one morning. Dawn hadn't yet brightened the sky, but the birds were starting to rustle overhead. Will stirred his campfire to life and heated a pot of coffee. As the sky silvered, he noticed a deer track that led downhill. He didn't remember seeing it when he made camp. It reminded him of Melissa's voice from the dream. *Deer probably pass through here on the way to water*, he thought, though he knew there was no river below this section of woods. *What the hell*, he said to himself as he poured the last of his coffee over the campfire, rolled his sleeping bag, and slung his pack over his shoulder. Then he picked his way carefully down the narrow path, sliding and hanging onto saplings as it grew steep. Within a few dozen paces, he found himself in old growth forest with a high, dense canopy, and the mist dampened the forest sounds. As the sun came up, a beam of light sliced through the haze. Will's imagination made even the slightest rustle in the branches overhead sound like voices.

"*Sh-sh-sh-she's waiting by the river . . .*"

It's only the wind, he told himself, though he scanned the woods on all sides as he continued slip-sliding down the path.

The leaves rattled, whispering encouragement.

He wandered lost until the fog burned away and the whispering leaves gave way to the sound of water babbling over rocks. Will's heart leapt, and he ran as best he could down the steep rutted, root-strewn, nearly indistinguishable path. He slipped and slid toward the gurgling water.

Melissa whispered in his head, "*I'm waiting, Daddy.*"

At the river's edge he saw her sitting on a smooth rock. He caught his breath, and hot tears filled his eyes.

"*I waited for you, Daddy.*"

"Oh, honey. Where have you been all this time?" Then he saw a rusted bit of bumper sticking out of the water and he knew. With joyous tears streaming down his face, he hugged her.

It was several months before anybody even realized Will was missing. When they found his body at the base of the cliff, there wasn't any flesh left. If his driver's license hadn't been in his backpack they'd have needed dental records to identify him. The surprise was finding his daughter's SUV, her body still inside, less than a dozen feet away. No one living could explain how the girl had driven into that remote section of the park. No roads had ever penetrated that deep into the woods, though if any natives had survived to tell the tale, the white men would have known of the ghost river that flowed there from the spirit world.

Nebula and the Wolf

Almost nineteen years old and on her own, Nebula had the whole world to explore (right after she checked on her mother). She stood on the filthy sidewalk outside the Greyhound bus station, backpack on her shoulders and suitcase by her side, her gingham dress see-through with age.

She was a picture standing there silhouetted in the sunshine. The man watched her taking her bearings. The bus station was his favorite place to watch. He was lean and rangy with the roadrunner shouting *Beep-Beep!* from his T-shirt. He hid his eyes behind a cheap pair of sunglasses and pulled his long greasy hair into a ponytail. She stood there. Looking this way and that. He could almost taste her sweet flesh already. He sidled up to her. "Can I help you, little girl?" he asked so low he was almost whispering in her ear. "You look lost."

Nebula stepped away from the man's hot breath. She noticed his dirty feet in duct-taped flip flops. Then her eyes lifted to meet his. "Uh . . . I just need to find . . ." But the trouble was, she needed to find everything: a place to stay, a job, something to eat, her mother.

"Town's this way," the man said, straightening up tall. "I'm walking that way if you'd like to join me. Name's Wolfie." The string bean of a man fidgeted while the girl took a long deep breath. He chuckled. "How do you like the taste of our beautiful LA smog?" The girl's eyes met his and sent a delicious little chill down his spine.

There wasn't any way Wolfie could know that Nebula's deep breath had allowed her to reach down through the concrete with a psychic grounding cord to connect with the earth. It was a little trick she'd learned listening to guided meditations she found at the library. Connecting with a place that way let her tune in to what was going on around her a lot faster. She picked up her suitcase and turned the way the man was facing. She wanted to dip her toes in the ocean first thing, but this guy was a sign. No doubt about it.

"Let me carry your case," he said and led her past the LAPD and into Skid Row.

As they walked, Nebula's eyes filled with tears seeing the condition of the homeless people lining the sidewalks. The man walking beside her didn't seem to notice her crying. He was clearly a predator, but Nebula always followed the signs, even when they looked like they were pointing her into trouble. She wiped her eyes and played along. She knew this man would pick the spot when it was time, like the redneck boys back home who'd been wreathed in the same swirling, malevolent colors this man showed when they followed her home and would have attacked her if the neighbor's big dog hadn't come snarling and barking at them. Deep iridescent reds and blacks broadcast their intent. This man—"What's your name again?"—his aura said "hunger." Nebula knew that she was the tidbit making him drool.

"Wolfgang—everybody calls me Wolfie."

"I'm Nebula." She refrained from adding "pleased to meet you." She wasn't pleased to meet him, but she'd known she'd meet someone like him. There was always someone. This time, it happened to be Wolfie. She fingered her mother's charm bracelet as she walked, stretching her legs to match the man's long stride.

"Where you comin' from?" Wolfie asked. Just passing the time, you understand, but he wanted to put the girl at her ease.

"Texas."

"First time in California?"

"No."

He looked down at her, checking his initial assessment of her as a girl on her own. "Looking to see the sights, or you got somebody out here you're coming to see?"

"My mother."

Wolfie nodded. That'd throw a wrench in the works if the kid had family to come looking, best to make her disappear quick—before they even knew she'd gotten off the bus. If he was real lucky, they didn't know she was coming—would never even miss her. He'd just spend a little time sussing her out first. "Would you let me buy you some lunch? I don't expect you've had much to eat coming all the way from Texas. A bag of chips or so? Am I right?" When he talked to her, he turned sideways crab-walking along beside her, long limbs gesticulating.

He put Nebula more in mind of a spider than a wolf. She said, "Sure, that'd be nice."

The wolf-spider-man led her into a greasy spoon café. "Best burgers in town," He said, holding the glass door wide for her.

The air in the place was heavy, not just with the things everyone noticed, the grease and the decades-old nicotine stench, but with exhaustion, decay, deceit. Nebula picked at her fries and sipped her Coke. She couldn't eat the burger. Her mind's-eye showed her maggots crawling under the bun. "I can't eat the burger," she said. "Want it?"

"I ate earlier. You go on and eat up, darlin'," Wolfie said. "I'm flush today. Had a good day at the track yesterday." He leered at her.

A fly landed below Nebula's left ear, out of Wolfie's line of sight, and she cocked her head ever-so-slightly in the insect's direction. To Wolfie she said, "Thank you. I'm just not feeling too good after so many hours on the road. It was kind of you to offer, though. I need to get going now. It's a ways to my mother's place."

"Oh? Where's she live at? Maybe I can point you in the right direction."

She hated to do it, but Nebula agreed to let the guy accompany her at least part of the way. He paid for the meal she didn't eat, and they left. Nebula blinked and inhaled smog, coughing a little. The menace of the man began to feel too close.

"Where does your mother live, Sweetheart?"

Nebula made up an address.

Wolfie chuckled to himself but played along. "That's too far to walk, you know. You got money for a bus ride? I could show you the stops."

"Thanks, I used to live here. I know the way." She didn't want to tell Wolfie that her mother could be on any one of these Skid Row sidewalks. She wanted to check the shelters first.

Wolfie kept pace with her, fighting the urge to just yank her into an alley. There'd be plenty left for the guy in Tijuana.

Nebula knew she was going to have to take drastic action. The fly had warned her that girls disappeared around Wolfie.

Sure enough, as they started down an empty block lined with boarded up windows and doors, Wolfie sidled up close, wrapped his long arm around her, covered her mouth with his other hand, and shoved her into an alley where broken glass sparkled like the Milky Way on the asphalt. He crab-walked them quickly to the far side of a dumpster and forced her onto a pile of boxes. Somewhere along the way, a knife materialized in his hand, and he showed it to her while the weight of him held her down. Foul breath chuffed out of his mouth which seemed suddenly too large, with too many teeth. He drooled and his greasy hair touched her face as he worked at the buttons on his jeans, saying, "You almost made me cream in my jeans, girlie. Couldn't wait no more."

"I'm sorry," she said.

Wolfie laughed. "My, aren't we polite." He stuck his hand between her legs, clearing the path, as it were. That's when he relaxed his grip just a little on her wrists and wobbled on one elbow so he could fiddle with his dick trying to find were to stick it.

And that was the moment Nebula released a burst of energy—she didn't know what else to call it—just energy. It pulsed out from the center of her, the very core of her being. It was a force powerful enough to throw Wolfie through the air to the far end of the alley and knock him out with all his manly glory on display for the paramedics when they came.

Nebula picked herself up, arranged her panties, dusted off her dress, pulled on her backpack, picked up her suitcase, and felt her charm bracelet to make sure she hadn't lost it.

A rat ran along the edge of the asphalt where the brick wall met the gutter. She stopped every few feet to rub at her face. "Miss! Uh-hum . . . MISS!" she squeaked.

Nebula turned a smile toward the polite little creature. "Well, hello, Mrs. Rat."

"What was that you did, Miss? Knocked me over, it did."

Nebula said. "I'm sorry for the trouble."

"That's alright, Miss. We're all okay, and that fellow had it coming. Seen him down this way before, we have."

"Say, Mrs. Rat, do you know a lot of the people who live down here on the sidewalks?"

Trust Issues

"This is Susan Stallings reporting for CCWN from outside the Holy Shepard's Episcopal Church in Ellington, Texas, where Texas' first transgender candidate for the US House of Representatives has been taken following a shooting incident. Facts are still emerging . . ."

"I seen it when it happened," shouted someone off camera.

"Haul that sum-bitch out here so we can finish the job," came another call.

The reporter said, "Cut, Sam. Let's get some eye-witness accounts. Take a few shots of the signs." She pointed to a hastily lettered poster board placard that read "God decides if you're A MAN OR A WOMEN." Another read, "No Trans 4 Congress," and a third said "Johnson = ABOMINATION."

Several reporters stood at the front of an angry crowd blocking the front and side entrances of the tiny church.

Sam kept his camera rolling as the reporters shouted toward the church: "Isabel! Are you alright?"; "Candidate Johnson, give us a sign!"; "Is the candidate alright? Does she—he—uh—*they* need medical attention?"

A police cruiser, driven by an officer from a neighboring town pulled up, siren wailing, lights flashing. The officer approached another uniformed man guarding an area in a parking lot across the street that was cordoned off with yellow tape. The officer on guard lifted the tape and pointed at the Sheriff who was holding forth in the center of the parking lot. Around him, the local police force, all five of them, and various sheriff's deputies bustled around accomplishing very little.

"Busby, got-dammit," the Sheriff bellowed, "take this idiot to the jail. The FBI can get him from there. Looks like they won't get here before tonight."

"Yessir." A young deputy got into the driver's seat of a cop car with flashing lights. A wild-eyed man, his bottom lip bulging with snuff, occupied the back seat. The pearl snaps on his denim shirt were open, exposing a sweaty, hairless chest. He stared straight ahead.

"Sheriff, I'm Jake Flowers. They sent me over from Middleton to lend a hand."

"Flowers. I don't know what you can do to help right now. We've got the shooter on the way to the jail for holding till the FBI gets here to collect him. Wasn't any question about who did it."

Flowers took in the still angry crowd around the church. "How 'bout I wade in across the street—take a few statements and send them home?"

"We all saw what happened. I don't know what a bunch of eye witness accounts to the same damned thing is going to accomplish. That queer, or L-X-Y-Z, or whatcha callit candidate for Congress was just getting up to make his . . . her . . . what-the-hell-ever . . . the candidate gets up and starts speaking and these fools start hollering."

"The crowd?"

"That's right. Next thing you know, Willard Filmore takes a potshot at the candidate with his .22."

"How'd he get in here with a gun?"

"Humph. Wasn't inside the area where the speech was taking place, was he? Pulled up outside the fence over there and stood up on the roof of his truck to take aim."

"You're shitting me."

"Nope. Then the dang fool turned hisself in. No way we could've got him so quick without shooting him otherwise. He was real sorry he actually hit somebody."

"What the hell?"

"Fool was liquored up—acting like some cowboy on television. He's so damn dumb, he'll probably get off if he pleads plum stupid. But you have to tell me what that *person* thought was going to happen, coming here to speak. He, I mean she, knows we're prejudiced against blacks here. Hell, he grew up here. And he's a *fairy* on top of it. Willard just got the first shot off. The rest of 'em was fixin' to get in terrible trouble some kind of way. Seems like he saved them all from a night in jail."

"Oh!" Pastor Sharon clutched her pearls and jumped when her right cheekbone came into contact with the candidate's left elbow as she turned away from the slim gap in the curtains. She hadn't realized that Isabel Johnson, candidate for the thirty-eighth Texas congressional district was standing behind her.

"Sorry, Pastor. I thought you heard me." Johnson, an athlete turned academic had a voice like honey—low-pitched but silky soft.

The little pastor's helmet of hair looked slightly off-center. She took the candidate's arm and marched them to a darkened hallway away from the windows. Nostrils flaring, the pastor recalled her own years as a middle-school principal. Scowling up over the rims of her glasses she said, "Dr. Johnson, these rednecks have already taken a shot at you, and it sounds like the rest of them would rip you limb from limb. Do you have a death wish?"

Chastened, the candidate stared at their feet. "No, of course not."

"I've called for help. We may be able to get you away from here before any of them know you're gone."

"I've worked a few tough crowds, Pastor. I could just walk out the door and give my speech. That's what I'm here for, after all."

"That's a bad idea. Our little police force can't do anything at all to protect you. They sympathize with this crowd, and frankly, I wouldn't be surprised if they turned a blind eye to further violence."

The candidate wasn't convinced. "The news crews have arrived. The eyes of the world are watching."

"You don't understand what the people of this town are capable of. Trust me. You need to get out of here and let the news of the shooting play for a day or two."

As if on cue, a slight figure emerged from the shadowed hallway to the sacristy.

Pastor Sharon started.

"Jumpy today, Sharon?" the voice whispered.

"Nell. Thank the good Lord you are finally here. Isabella, this is Nell. She's going to get you out of here before anyone knows you're gone."

Johnson, all six-foot-two of them, inhaled deeply and frowned. "*This* tiny person is my salvation?"

Nell, who might have weighed a hundred pounds dripping wet, looked like bone and gristle wrapped in combat gear. Her worn-leather face was framed by wispy gray hair gathered into a braid. A sleeveless black tank top revealed sagging breasts and faded tattoos. She looked at Sharon. "*This* the valuable asset you want me to sneak out of here?"

"We're getting off to a great start." Johnson turned to the pastor and said, "Really, you shouldn't have. I'll just take my chances outside." They pivoted on a custom size-14 Jimmy Choo pump.

The tenacious little pastor ran to block the door. "I did not save you so you could sacrifice yourself to that mob."

"What do you care?"

"I sincerely believe that you are the right person for the job. We need a voice for all the people who aren't being heard because of idiots like that guy who shot your assistant."

"And you called for this barely civil person to whisk me away on the back of her Harley?"

Nell bristled. "I don't need this, Sharon. And fuck you very much, candidate. I'd rather finish cutting my grass." She started back the way she had just come.

"I'm ashamed of you, Isabel Johnson. I thought your platform was all about not judging people. Yet here you stand casting judgment on a woman you just met. Nell is probably the most capable person in three counties when it comes to sneaking out from under the noses of the law."

"I didn't mean . . ."

Nell interrupted, "How the hell is it just the two of you in here? Where are your people, candidate?"

"There were only two," Johnson answered. "My PA, Stephanie . . ." they choked up and sniffled, "got shot, and while everyone else ran around like headless chickens, Tom, my PR guy, was doing CPR, and Sharon here pulled me across the street and into the church."

"Where's Tom now?"

"He went in the ambulance with Stephanie."

"Un-fucking-believable," said Nell. "So, what do you expect me to do, Sharon?"

"Just get the candidate out of here."

"What, run her out to the Shell station?" Nell asked.

"My pronouns are they, them, and their."

Nell cast a sideways glance at Isabel Johnson. "That purple silk suit and heels kind of stand out around here."

"Work it out on the way, just go!" The pastor made a shooing gesture.

"Am I doing this out of the goodness of my heart?"

"I will cover your fee." Johnson said, slipping their handbag over a shoulder. "Which way?"

Nell turned on her hobnail boots and bowed low, sweeping an arm through the shadows she'd walked out of. "Right this way, candidate."

A door led outside from Pastor Sharon's office, or sacristy, to give the tiny room the grand title she preferred, but that door was so rarely used that almost no one knew it was there. From outside, it was entirely obscured by a Ligustrum hedge. Nell put a finger to her lips as she eased the door open and ducked into the foliage. As she prepared to sprint across the narrow span of lawn to the next row of shrubs at the edge of the property, she heard Isabel Johnson cursing.

"Spiders! I hate spiders."

"Shhh," Nell hissed. "I'd slip those shoes off if I were you. We're going to have to run."

"Shit!"

Nell whipped around and grabbed the lanky candidate's hand. "Not now, drama queen. Not a sound." She looked at the pointy-toed pumps dyed to match the candidate's orchid-colored suit.

Isabel slipped out of the shoes, picked them up with two fingers, and nodded, indicating that they were ready.

Nell led the way across a strip of sunlit lawn, into the shade of a hackberry tree, and finally into the hedge running along the fence line. Once Isabel crouched beside her, Nell said, "We have to go through this barbed wire, then sprint to the front of the neighbor's house. My car is parked at the curb."

If you discounted the fact that a tiny shred of purple silk had hooked on the barbed wire, and that old Mrs. Spencer claimed to have seen a tiny hoodlum in camo and a very tall colored person in purple run past her side window, then the sprint to Nell's car could be called a success.

"Strap in," Nell ordered.

Isabell made a face and put a hand to their nose.

"What? Not fancy enough for you?" The 1975 Alpha Romeo Spider had sun-blistered paint and a ragged cloth top. Its torn upholstery carried a faint aroma of cat piss.

Isabell, eyes raised, silently whispered the twenty-third Psalm.

In spite of its appearance, the car roared to life, and Nell's face softened into a smile. "I haven't had this baby long enough to worry about her looks. Engine's better than it was new, though."

The next block over, Deputy Jake Flowers from Middleton and Susan Stallings from the County Communiqué Website News both heard the rumble as Nell's car started, then ran rapidly through the gears on the way to the highway.

Just then, Pastor Sharon opened the door of the Holy Shepherd's Church and stepped out. A hush fell over the crowd. Placards came to attention and all eyes turned toward her.

"The candidate is fine, but for security reasons, they prefer to have me deliver a statement."

Coarse remarks started flying as Flowers jogged to his cruiser. He was pulling away from the curb when the reporter latched onto the passenger door handle. He rolled down the window and she yanked the door open and jumped in.

In a barely controlled voice, Flowers said, "Ma'am, get out of my car."

"Arrest me when we're done. If you don't hurry, though, you're going to lose them."

The officer's jaw clenched. "Put your seatbelt on," he said and flipped on the lights. He turned the siren on at the first major crossroads and reached for the radio handset but hesitated and didn't pick it up.

"What? Call it in," Stallings said.

"And say what? I don't even know what kind of car I'm chasing. This is probably a wild goose chase."

The cruiser caught air going over a little hump of a bridge on the narrow road that ran parallel to Main Street. The reporter gripped the edges of her seat.

Flowers said, "Get ready to look right when we get to the bridge over the highway. I'll look left."

"And look for . . . ?"

"Somebody speeding. Roll down your window. We'll hear 'em first."

"AAAAAAAAAAHHHH," Isabel Johnson screamed as Nell's roadster took the right turn onto the highway feeder on two wheels.

Nell cackled like the maniac she became any time she had a legitimate reason to really drive.

"I don't want to di-i-i-i-e," Johnson screamed. They gripped the insubstantial frame of the convertible top while stomping at the floor as if there were a brake pedal there.

Nell didn't hear. She was timing her freeway entrance to place them between eighteen-wheelers.

"There!" shouted the reporter. "They just got on between two trucks."

Officer Flowers yanked the wheel making a hard U-turn to get back to the feeder road.

"Ow!" Stallings hit her head on the door frame. "You might have warned me."

"Sorry." Flowers knew he was going to be in big trouble when it came out that he'd taken a reporter on a car chase, but it was the only way he was going to catch them.

"Officer," Stallings said once the windows were rolled up and she could speak without shouting. "Why are you chasing this car? I know why I'm here—I want a scoop, but what do you get out of catching the candidate?"

"I've got a feeling the candidate is not there by choice. Someone has already taken a shot at 'em. I think it is a kidnapping in progress."

Stallings sat back in her seat, incredulous. *That* possibility had not crossed her mind.

Nell jerked the little car into the middle lane inches from the shiny chrome bumper of a Peterbilt.

"AAAAAAIEEEE!" Isabel screamed. "What in the hell are you doing? You're supposed to be saving me, not getting me killed!"

"I saw flashing lights."

"I surrender! Give me to the cops. They'll protect me."

Nell turned a hard look toward the passenger seat. "You haven't heard the stories, then."

"What stories?"

"In Ellington, people commit suicide with *two* shots to the head."

Isabel thought about that for a minute.

Nell could tell when the penny dropped. "Why have you even put yourself in this position? Seems pretty damned stupid to paint a target on yourself this way."

"You wouldn't understand."

Nell smirked. "Seriously? Have you seen me?"

Isabel laughed. "Okay. I grew up not far from Ellington— way out in the country. I know all about the bigoted redneck attitudes here. My daddy gave his life for this country and my mama scrubbed those s.o.b.'s toilets to send me to school. I still have family here. I want to see the under-represented folk—the working people, not just the LGBTQ community, but everybody these bigots take advantage of—get a voice."

Nell nodded, and they rode in silence for several miles.

"Where are you taking me, then, if the Ellington police are that corrupt?" Isabel asked.

"The college. You'll be safe there."

"Why are you doing this?"

"Me? Adrenaline junkie. Don't have much use for people. Should have been a moonshiner, but I was born in the wrong time."

"So, you live around here?"

"Way out in the woods."

"How do you get by?"

"Shade tree mechanic. Got some chickens. Grow me some vegetables—a little pot."

"Why are you helping me?"

"M-O-N-E-Y, baby! Plus, it's a chance to drive like that bat out of hell I was born to be!"

Flowers switched off the lights.

"Why'd you do that?" Stallings asked.

"I know where they are, and I don't want to spook them."

Fifteen miles down the road in the neighboring college town, the battered little sports car squirted like a watermelon seed spat from the mouth of a behemoth truck onto the exit ramp.

Flowers spotted them crossing an overpass just after he passed the exit. "Shit!"

"Is that them?"

"Yeah. There's another exit up ahead. We'll have to get off there and make our way back."

"They'll be long gone by then."

"I think they'll be heading for the campus. If you're a praying person, now would be a good time. We're going to need some luck or divine intervention to find them."

Nell turned in under the stone archway that announced the entrance to Davy Crockett State University. The campus looked deserted, as it usually did on a Saturday.

"There's nobody here. What's Plan B, *Nell?*" Isabel spat their rescuer's name.

"Hang tight, *Isabel*." Nell's tone mirrored the candidate's, but her mouth spread in a delighted grin.

Sure enough, Nell's instinct proved correct, and on the far side of the campus, the parking lot of the stadium was teeming. Unfortunately, on this particular Saturday, it was not a crowd that could do much to help a political candidate on the run. Half the stadium parking lot was filled with school busses and high school students in a variety of band uniforms were being herded around the outside of the stadium by red-faced band directors. Several parents scowled in the direction of Nell's loud exhaust. The sound of drums and horns wafted out of the stadium.

Isabel looked at Nell, the question plain on their face.

"Well, hell," Nell said turning back onto University Parkway.

"Just take me to Dairy Queen and I'll call someone to come get me."

"Yeah. Alright."

Flowers was turning in through the DCSU entrance, windows lowered, listening for the distinctive rumble of the Alpha Romeo when Nell drove right past him going the opposite way.

"Crap!" He flipped on the lights and the siren as he wrenched his car around in a tight three-point turn.

"Warn me!" snapped Susan Stallings, rubbing the lump on the side of her head.

Nell said, "Shit."

"Just pull over. Get it over with," said Isabel.

"No fucking way. That is the same bastard that's been following us since Ellington. They'll lock me up and throw away the key." And she gunned it.

"Hold on," Flowers said.

"No shit, Sherlock."

"Crap, crap, crap," Nell muttered as she wracked her brain for a way to hide from the cop who was right behind her.

"Nell!" Isabell yelled and shoved Nell's right arm to avoid a silver dual-wheel pickup truck that shot out from a cross street. The car clipped the truck's bumper but made it past without slowing down.

A mile down the road, just after a sharp bend, they ran over a tack strip, and Nell was forced to stop.

"Get down low," she said and reached behind her seat.

"No, Nell. They will kill us both, and there won't be anybody to ask questions."

Isabel unfolded from the passenger seat of the little car, one Jimmy Choo at a time. Their hands were raised and steady as they faced three officers with weapons drawn.

Officer Flowers jumped out of the cruiser and ran. The scene in front of him would have been ludicrous if it hadn't been so deadly serious. A short fat officer was trying to place cuffs on Isabel Johnson, who was standing perfectly still. The officer became enraged when he couldn't reach Johnson's hands, so he kicked the legs out from under the candidate for the US House of Representatives.

"Hey, hey!" Flowers had his hand on his side-arm as he raced to intervene.

Susan Stallings filmed the whole thing with her iPhone.

They'd all taken their eyes off Nell. The driver of the silver pickup had stopped behind Flowers' car, and when Nell opened her door, while the uniformed officers and the reporter focused on Johnson, the man grabbed Nell's braided hair and yanked her out of the car. He clocked her with a solid left hook before dragging her to the line of police. "Here you go, boys. I caught this one for you." Under his breath, he muttered, "I hope that dyke has insurance."

"Call an ambulance, would you, Skeeter?" One of the uniforms said to another. "Just set 'er down there. She ain't goin' nowhere."

It took Officer Flowers a while to talk the local boys out of arresting Isabel, who stood silently in handcuffs, the knees of their suit ripped, their nose bleeding.

When the cuffs came off, Isabel turned to look for Nell.

Sharon Stallings' iPhone caught the candidate's stricken face in the perfect light as they said, "Where's Nell?" It ran on all the national news stations that night along with the story of candidate Johnson's very bad day, and that airplay alone is credited with making Isabel Johnson a household name.

In spite of Officer Jake Flowers', Susan Stallings', and US Congressional Representative Isabel Johnson's ceaseless efforts, Nell has yet to be found.

Blastoff

"9...8...7...," David Bowie's voice echoed through the astronauts' headphones. Dupree, who'd selected the first song for their blastoff soundtrack wiggled her fingers inside her oversized gloves while she waited, staring through layers of ghostly glassy reflections at the control panel lit up with green lights. All dials registering in the normal range. Butterflies tumbled over one another in her belly. The waiting was so exhausting and exhilarating all at the same time. She felt tired, but she wanted to be hyper-awake to record the moment of lift off, place it in her mental repository so she could watch it, live it, again and again.

"Come on. Really?" Evans, the other astronaut in the nose capsule jacked into the com with a loud click. "I am not blasting off into space, leaving my home world, to the sound of a cliché."

Well shit, thought Dupree. "Way to kill the buzz, sister." *Maybe I didn't want the next available seat on the Space Shuttle.*

Evans, ever the trailblazer, imagined *her* life as a grand adventure enlivened by innovation, never boring, never repetitive, never the same.

"You don't have to listen to my music. Didn't you program anything of your own to listen to?"

"Yes. Ambient noise. I want to hear what it sounds like to blast out of Earth's orbit with no drug-influenced bullshit whining through my headphones."

"Bo-o-oring," Dupree said and maneuvered the gauntlet on her left hand over to the switch that would make her music stream privately. She loved cliché and lived her life as if it were a Hollywood movie, with everything set to music. The butterflies in her belly effervesced. They'd practiced liftoff *ad nauseum* from the time they met at the center, so it ought to be routine. Still, there was always doubt, always worry that some cosmic law of averages would tag *their* flight to explode seventy-three seconds from launch to disperse their atoms across the Louisiana and Texas sky. But, of course, it would still be ages before the giant rocket boosters would ignite and send them into the sky.

Evans, meanwhile, lay quietly, emptying her mind of everything, willing her muscles to relax and her third eye to open so that she could feel every sensation, hear every sound, *be* the experience. Sure, she knew there was a chance this was the day she died, and she was pretty sure she was okay with that. Still, when her visualizations showed her old newsreels of rockets and Space Shuttles breaking apart, one on take-off, one on reentry, she was pulled back into her physical self, tensed, and had to start the relaxation process all over again. She was a giant turtle on her back, relaxing all the parts of her body—toes to fingertips—relaxing slowly up through her limbs and into the core of her body to her shoulders and neck. She surrendered control. Breathing in to slowly, slowly, hold, hold, hold, hold, and exha-a-a-a-a-a-a-ling. She heard the rumbling hum of the systems as they started one by one, guided by some white-shirted, black-tie-wearing geek in the control room, and she felt her essence vibrating in harmony—

"*TCH-CH-CH. . .*" The com made them both jump as it superseded Dupree's music, like the pilot on an airplane—interrupting just as the movie gets past the credits. Evans jumped, jerked unceremoniously from her meditation by the obnoxious sound. "Commander Evans, Lieutenant Dupree, we wish you a smooth flight. We'll be here watching and guiding you the whole way. Godspeed."

A second voice said "10 . . . ," and both women's heartbeats intensified at the sound of a thousand pounds of propellant flooding the combustion chambers. "9 . . . 8 . . . 7 . . ." They were looking at each other, wide-eyed, when at ". . . 6 . . ." the engines roared to life and the rocket began bucking and pulling at the bolts on the launchpad. And at "1 . . ." the solid boosters strapped to the main rocket ignited.

Dupree stared out the port in front of her—at first obscured by the steamy smoke of lift-off, then filled first with blue sky quickly darkening, then as the capsule tilted, with the earth below them rapidly receding. She felt her heart hammering in her chest—awed and expectant. She squealed, "EEEEEEEE! It's happening! Look at the size of everything down there!"

Evans ground her teeth. *All the preparation and expense of this trip and I'm stuck with Barbie for my copilot*, she thought. "Do you remember what you're supposed to do, Dupree?"

"Yes, Captain," Dupree said, with as much snark as she could muster. She was reaching for the switch that would enable their cameras to adjust their attitude when the first red light appeared on the control panel.

"Fuck, what's that?" Evans said.

"*TCH-CH-CH . . . Evans, Dupree, do you read?*" The control room chatterbox started shouting into their ears as master alarms went off and every light in the capsule started blinking, every horn sounded.

"Fuck, fuck, fuck." Dupree flailed her bulky gauntlets in every direction, wildly pushing buttons, trying to get something, anything, to reset the noisy alarms so she could think. The butterflies were gnawing their way out from the inside. She screamed, choking on snot and saliva like a rabid dog drowning in its own juices. A hissing sound built growing louder as the capsule tumbled out of control. Dupree vomited.

Evans had practically stopped her breathing, though she was fighting with the hammering of her pulse in her ears as she was slammed around in her suit. Dupree was screaming through the headset, but Evans fought the urge to slap the silly bitch. That would serve no purpose now. She had lived her life in control of every moment, and she'd be damned if her last ones would be spent trying to school a hysterical fashion-doll clone. She offered up a prayer for peace in the afterlife and repented a lifetime of sins wholesale. There was no time for an itemized list.

Bradly Harris yanked the heavy door aside and stared into two sets of frightened eyes squinting up from inside the capsule.

"Come on, ducks," he said and locked arms with the first one, who looked pale, but more-or-less in control. She got all the buckles undone without help and pushed up to clasp his arm. He helped her find her balance and turned back to repeat the process with the second woman, who had clearly freaked all the way out judging by the state of the inside of her helmet. "Out you come. That's it," he said, coaxing her gently into a standing position after unclasping her seat belts. He reached for a towel for this second woman.

Dupree wobbled into a standing position, but hadn't the strength to hold it, and Bradly caught her just as she was about to fall and guided her to a rolling office chair where he helped her off with her helmet. She stared at him, confused by his bright red plaid shirt.

She's right out of it, Bradly thought, registering the shock on the woman's face. "I'm your technician. I didn't have a chance to grab my lab coat when the alarms went off."

"Where. . . ?"

"It's a simulation. You just experienced the final recorded moments of the Space Shuttle Challenger's last flight."

Evans removed her helmet, in control again and mad as hell. "I'd like my money back. That was not the space flight I paid for. And. . ."

Bradly interrupted, "I'm sorry you were not happy with your flight, Ms. Evans." He consulted a clipboard hanging by the door. "Your coupon entitled you to a *random* Space Shuttle flight. You signed a disclaimer stating that you understood that you might draw any of the recorded Space Shuttle flights, including disastrous flight STS-51-L, the 25th Space Shuttle mission—the Columbia's final flight."

Lucinda Dupree, meanwhile, gingerly worked at the fittings for her gauntlets, her soiled helmet on the floor at her feet. She said, "That was certainly a shock to my system . . . Guess I'm not so good in a crisis."

Bradly disconnected some cords from her suit.

She said, "How often does this happen?"

"Not often," he said. "Always takes me by surprise too. I went down to the restroom. Thought I had a little longer. Left my coat in the break room."

The other one, Evans, rattled around, and Bradly turned to her. "Easy there, Ms. Evans. Let me get your wires disconnected."

"I think you need to get your manager in here. I want a refund."

Bradly pretended not to hear and turned back to the other woman. "Here let me help you out of that suit." He unclasped a boot, then wiggled it back and forth, rocking it from heel to toe.

"Did you hear me? Mountain man? I'm talking to you."

"I'll be right with you, Ms. Evans," he said. "I'm . . . almost . . . done here." He sat down hard on his behind as Dupree's second boot slid off with a sucking noise like a cow pulling her foot out of the mud.

"Thank you," Dupree said, looking embarrassed that the other woman was making such a fuss. "I can take it from here." She touched the wild, puke-infused birds' nest on her head and offered a tiny grin.

Bradly knew the clients had no idea how much effort it took to clean the suits and helmets on a good day, let alone after one of those full-on bodily-fluids episodes. The gear this woman used would have to be pulled out of circulation—part of the reason these adventures were so expensive. The team who looked after the suits would practically have to rebuild this helmet to sanitize it. Bradly had had a feeling this wasn't going to be a fun sort of flight when these two were suiting up. It probably wouldn't have mattered what simulation they'd drawn. They were never going to be friends by the end of the journey. Evans had been pissy and looking for something to complain about the whole time. The gauntlets were too stiff—Bradly had WD-40'd them—the boots were too tight—Bradly'd filled them with talcum powder and found her a thinner pair of socks—and the volume control for her headphones was wonky—Bradly had had to run a new wire for that. Dupree, meanwhile, had been excited and nice, clearly ready for a good time. They'd drawn badly and were not compatible at all, but as the last clients of the day, there were no others waiting who might be convinced to trade places with one of these ladies. Couples and families talked to each other, compared notes on their journeys, had a good time—even on the final Challenger flight. Not these two.

Bradley tried to make small talk. "Did you know that there are some people who actually request the Challenger's last flight? Just last week, these two brothers came in and they were hooting and hollering and high-fiving when it was over . . ."

"I did *not* ask for the Challenger's last flight. I asked for space flight. That one never got to space," said Evans.

"It's not normally allowed with coupon deals, but I'm sure we can refund a portion of what you paid today—give you a credit toward your next visit."

"I want my money back."

"The ad did say, 'Adversity Brings Us Together: The Ultimate Bonding Experience.' We didn't advertise this as a chill, laid-back trip into orbit." The coupon deals were aimed at singletons paired up at random. It had become a dating fad. People enjoyed the thrill of getting to know new people in a safe but extreme environment. You could really get acquainted very quickly.

The percentage of positive outcomes outweighed the negatives like this one. The bookings increased, so the administrators loved it, but they weren't the ones who opened the capsule and helped the clients out when it was over. No, Bradly did that. He'd been a lab tech in this job for three years, and he'd seen hundreds of couples into and out of the pod. He could tell how the flight would go for them before he ever closed the hatch and pushed start on the adventure. He lumped the people who came in alone into two categories: extreme introverts with no social skills or assholes who had no friends. The introverts in their extreme form were demure by nature if not by form, and the assholes were either bullies or fear-biters, mad at the world over everything or terrified and delusional, and none of them knew anything about teamwork. Still, Space Shuttle Speed Dating was a sort of teambuilding exercise that could result in amazingly powerful bonds. The operative word there was *could*.

"That's about what I expected," Evans said. She crossed her arms and curled her lip. "I would like a cash refund." She tried to force a stiff clasp open—nearly ripping the skin of her suit in the process.

Bradly scuttled around to her side. "Ms. Evans—here—let me help you out of that suit." He took hold of the left sleeve and yanked, shucking the disgruntled woman's shoulders out of the heavy Kevlar suit and spinning her around. "There, now." He steadied her and pointed her in the direction of the locker room. "I'll get some forms together for you to register your complaint while you get dressed."

She swung back toward him. "I want to speak to your manager."

"I'm sorry, Ms. Evans. That won't be possible. I'm on my own right now."

"Then dial up another flight and let me go again right now —on my own, this time." She gave Dupree a withering look.

"Can't do that either, ma'am. Everyone's gone home."

The quiet one, Lucinda Dupree chimed in, "What should I do with the suit? Just leave it here?" She stepped over it on tiptoe, holding her nose as if it were a dead thing.

"That's fine," Bradly said. "I'll take care of it." Dupree turned toward the dressing room but he called after her, "You can claim for a disappointing ride, too, Ms. Dupree."

"Oh, that's sweet of you, Bradly, but I knew it might be the Challenger explosion. I've always felt sad for them."

Bradly nodded. It was just another day at the Museum of Aerospacial History's Space Shuttle Experience.

Evans exited the dressing room to find Bradly with a bottle of disinfectant spray in one hand and a wad of paper towels in the other.

"Ah, Ms. Evans," he said. "Here are those papers I promised you." He handed her a fat envelope. "Instructions are inside." He knew the forms would take her so long to fill out that she'd probably drop the claim and never come back.

With a twisted sour lemon expression, she grabbed the papers and marched out of the lab. No word of thanks, but then Bradly hadn't expected any.

Lucinda Dupree emerged with her freshly washed hair forming a wild halo of curls around her face.

Bradly reached into a drawer in his workbench and pulled out several half-price coupons. He said, "Ask for me when you come back."

The Cave

Most epic adventures don't start out with an application and an insurance waiver, but, hell, most epic adventures were less than epic at the end of the day. At least, that was my take on them. It was damned hard to get my adrenals working anymore. I'd been everywhere, seen everything. I'd killed for a living, and saved lives for a living. Point me at a fire or a fire fight, and I was your gal.

In my time off, I was generally bored out of my mind, so I traveled, skydiving one month, scuba diving the next. That's why when I saw the advertisement in *Soldier of Fortune* for a spelunking team forming up to explore a newly discovered cave system, I applied. The application and insurance waiver were formalities. I knew one of the guys putting the trip together. I'd pulled his ass out of a jam in Afghanistan, and he vouched for me. Insurance? I hadn't been insurable my entire adult life because of the crazy shit I got up to. Insurance companies don't like adrenaline junkies.

It was a five-day trip—a day to hike in, a day to hike out, and three days in the cave. The geologists knew the cavern system was big, but not how big, so it was an exploratory mission. We should have already turned back by the start of the third day, but we'd passed through some incredible giant crystal formations and gotten photographs that were bound to find their way into *National Geographic,* so we'd made the collective decision to go a little bit further. We'd just had our breakfast of energy bars and water and were gathering our gear when the quake started.

I grabbed my buddy and towed him out of the cavern our camp was in. I was close to an opening that led off in a direction we hadn't explored yet, and that's what saved us. We were the only two members of the six-person team who made it out. The psych evals at the end said I'd been hallucinating, but I could have sworn I saw that cave close on the team like a giant mouth. And when it rumbled, it sounded like laughter.

I haven't felt a rush like that since my parachute jammed on my first solo jump.

Engineering the Apocalypse

The old man commanded the cheeseboard. His companion, Emily Preston, a slight figure in a wheelchair, would nod at the Cotswold or the gruyere and he'd feed it to her. Her nurse had helped her into a glittery blouse and taken a night off for the first time in six months. The blouse gave off far more light than Emily's face, which was pale with nearly translucent skin. Her waist was covered by a faux fur blanket. Her hair, though pulled up tight and sprayed into place, looked thin. It was her first night out since the accident, the first time she'd felt lucid enough by evening to go out. She was forty-seven years old, but she looked ninety.

Trays of canapés circulated around the room, and the old man, by dent of his extraordinary girth, dissuaded casual nibblers from approaching his end of the buffet. People stole glances at them from nearby tables, but no one could hear their conversation—if you could call it that. The old man spoke softly bending close to the woman's ear, and she replied with nods and scowls—the only means of communication that remained to her since the accident that had all but killed her. Robbed of her career in an instant, Emily had gone from high-powered stockbroker to invalid in one fateful moment. Her lawyer, the old man, had taken charge and helped her with the hard decisions that her son Tommy was too young to make. She'd been so out of it on medications she couldn't have made business decisions herself. She didn't know how they would have managed without the old man.

He whispered in her ear, "Tommy's a born fighter." He'd told her earlier that week that the money from the settlement was not going to last the year, and it certainly wasn't going to pay for Tommy's college. Her insurance had maxed-out with the hospital bills, the drugs, the skilled nurses, the physiotherapy, the modifications to the house. Now she was beginning to wonder how much she was paying for the old man's fine concierge services.

She nodded. To anyone looking, she appeared lucid. The doctors had finally balanced the cocktail of drugs she took so that she could spend longer stretches of time awake.

"You know it isn't always some bully goading him into fights at school."

She looked at her lap.

"Kid's like a berserker. Push the right button and he'll fight to the death."

She scowled.

"I mean that metaphorically, of course, Em."

Her eyes filled with tears, and the corners of her mouth turned down.

Pristine in his silk shirt and waistcoat, gold watch chain artfully draped around his great round middle, the old man said, "He'll be fine, Em. I'll see to that. Let him do this for you. Pretty soon, sacking groceries isn't going to cover the medical bills."

Her tears spilled out, and he made a show of gently wiping them away. Her approval in front of an audience was essential. Emily's son Tommy could set the boxing world on fire with the right manager, but at seventeen he needed his only parent to sign a release.

Finally, she nodded.

"Fine. That's just fine Em. I've got the papers in the car." He lifted two fingers to signal the waiter drifting by with a champagne tray.

Tommy Preston was good-looking—six-foot-two with sandy blond hair and ripped—a surfer to melt the hearts of the betting public. His good looks would draw millions out of the white establishment if he lived up to his promise in the ring. The old man built the boy's reputation quickly with carefully selected opponents and he made sure the right people were looking every time a brown-skinned fighter hit the canvas at Tommy's feet. "The Angel" seemed an innocent moniker at first, but the old man's strategy soon became apparent.

Tommy was sitting in the old man's office cooling off after training one afternoon when the phone rang.

"I don't know, Carlos. He's just a kid." The old man made a wide-eyed open-mouthed gesture and pointed at the phone. His voice stayed smooth and even. "Give us another year. Your boy has what, twenty-five pounds on him?" He gestured as if reeling in a big fish. He had to make sure the hook was well and truly set. "You do that." He disconnected and jumped out of his chair and did a little cha-cha-cha.

"Who was that?" Tommy jumped up, excited without knowing what had happened.

"Carlos Mendoza. Diaz's manager. They've been watching you. He wants a fight."

"No fucking way! El Diablo?" Tommy bounced on the balls of his feet, punched the air, and whooped.

"Easy, killer. He weighs damn-nearly two-hundred pounds. Your one-seventy-five ain't gonna get it. I don't care how fast you are."

The match was eight months coming, time for Tommy to bulk up, time for the old man to whip the sports commentators into a frenzy over "The Angel" fighting "El Diablo," a lightning-fast Mexican named Eduardo Diaz who was on track to become the cruiserweight champion. The fight was billed as "The Apocalypse." Vendors sold haloes and horns, but anyone could tell who backed which fighter without those props. The racial lines were clearly drawn. All the city's off-duty police were hired to keep the crowd under control the night of the fight.

In the dressing room, Tommy said, "You placed the bets?"

"Of course. The win. The fight to finish by round six. A knockout." The old man didn't tell the kid he'd actually bet on El Diablo to win with a KO by round six. His work here was nearly done. The odds were slanting heavily in Tommy's favor, so when the kid went down, he'd be rich.

Tommy nodded.

Rounds one, two, and three looked close, and the old man found himself sweating in the front row next to Emily, who'd insisted on coming, though he'd tried to dissuade her. In the end he'd thought, *What the hell? Maybe it'll kill her when the kid gets knocked out.*

The bell rang at the start of the fourth round, and El Diablo came out of his corner slow. Tommy's fans went wild as he laid into the Mexican with a barrage of jabs to the body, but El Diablo had drawn Tommy in using Mohammad Ali's old rope-a-dope, and when the kid was nearly spent, El Diablo's lightning-fast right hook followed by a series of left jabs sent Tommy staggering across the ring. The ref called the round.

The old man was on his feet yelling. He ran over and whispered in Tommy's ear, "Next time he clocks you, go down."

"What?"

The bell sounded for round five.

Go Down? Tommy shook his head. *That* made him mad. He caught a second wind and moved like a dancer, and to quote one commentator, "The Angel rained down on El

Diablo with the full force of Heaven bringing him *down* in Round Five."

The old man flopped around in distress beside Emily, but she was looking around to catch the eye of a bookie across the room who grinned and gave her a thumbs up. She smiled for the cameras, and her nurse wheeled her back to greet her son. The old man was left to his own devices.

With increased periods of lucidity, Emily's stockbroker brain had returned, and it was only natural for her to want to hedge her bets.

#*ExclusionZone*

She'd gone in to feed the animals. At last count, there were fifteen dogs, thirty-two cats, twelve chickens, a few goats, and one small pig.

On this cold night, she was dragging a sled with a hundred pounds of dog food, fifty pounds of cat food, a case of canned sardines, and ten pounds of rice. She had a portable water purifier and a camp stove back in the tent. She wasn't supposed to be there, but she couldn't *not* look after the animals.

She'd cut through a couple of pastures and crossed a barbed wire fence on foot to enter at a place where there weren't any guards. It had taken her almost two hours. At least the government didn't patrol the entire fence line. Nobody would be out on a night like this anyway.

"They're predicting two feet of snow," Cathy had said as she helped Jill tie the food and supplies onto the sled.

"We'll be fine," Jill said.

"Why are you risking your life to do this, Jill?" Cathy asked. "You'll freeze to death *and* die of radiation poisoning."

"I'm not going to freeze, Cathy." Jill patted her new sub-zero sleeping bag and winked. "The animals stick close. They pile up at night and keep me warm."

"You look awful. Please come home," Cathy begged.

"I can't just leave those animals to die. I'm the only one who even cares that they're out there."

"And if you die, your skinny carcass will only feed them for about one day." Cathy was getting shrill. "We'll get the Animal Welfare people to come."

"I called them. Remember?"

"Then bring the animals out."

"How, Cathy? I'm not the Pied Piper, and we can't get within miles of where I'm camped with a car. We'd be arrested for trying."

"There has to be a way."

"Let me know when you think of it. Meanwhile, I need to get back there before the storm hits."

"You are out of your mind. I hope you don't die."

Cathy left quickly, and Jill was glad. She didn't want a long weepy goodbye.

At the campsite, a huge black dog wiggled out to meet her. A small pot-bellied pig grunted—poking his head through the tentflap.

"Chester!" She met the wiggling, whining furball in a crouching position with one knee sinking into a snowdrift. It tingled where the dog licked frozen skin. "I see you there, Claude," she said to the little pig. "Come on, let's feed everybody."

By the time the animals were all fed, and the food safely stowed in nets in the trees, Jill was exhausted. She felt too tired to make herself a cup of tea, but she knew she needed the warmth of it.

Sitting by the fire, cup in hand, she heard coyotes howling not far away. *They're too close*, she thought.

The woodland surrounded the power plant, and when the people had evacuated all the nearby homes, they'd left their pets to fend for themselves. The animals had instinctively gone to the woods—even farther from human help. The agencies with the ability to help were busy helping people. Pets were expendable.

As soon as she finished her tea, Jill crawled into the tent with three dogs, two cats and the pig. The rest settled down around the campsite.

"Claude," she said to the little pig as he snorted and rooted, settling into his spot, "don't you go out there tonight. The coyotes are close. They'll eat you up."

Sometime later she awoke to pitch blackness and the absolute quiet of new fallen snow. Quiet, that is, except for Chester growling by the tent flap.

"Shhh!" Jill swatted at the dog to come away from the flap and he shifted back to a protective position beside her.

Straining, she listened for any out-of-place sounds outside the tent. She stroked Chester and held her breath, praying none of the others in the tent made a noise. They huffed and puffed around her. Then she thought she heard something moving near the trees where the food nets hung.

It's winter, bears hibernate, she relaxed slightly, but it was only a matter of minutes before she grew impatient. *No help for it*. She heaved herself over to the tent flap to peek outside. The dogs crouched beside her, wagging their tails down low and looking for her command to charge.

A flashlight beam approached the clearing. Someone was following her sled tracks.

This is it, she thought. *They're onto me.*

A branch snapped and Jill clearly heard a voice whisper, "Shit!" which made the dogs rush out barking.

"Jill? Help!" the unmistakable voice called.

"Cathy? What are you doing out here?"

"I couldn't leave you alone in the cold."

Jill yanked her boots and parka on and made her way to release her partner from the pack of less-than-ferocious dogs wagging and sniffing at her.

"Does it look like I'm alone?" Jill asked. "Some guardians you are," she said to the dogs. Some of them looked sheepish.

Cathy shook her head.

"Come in. Let me stir up the fire. You must be freezing."

Once Cathy had warmed up, she said, "I want to film you and your animals tomorrow. Then we're going to put you all on YouTube."

The video went viral, and within the week, Jill went to jail, but not before a group of concerned citizens banded together to stop the military from using the animals for target practice. The whole pack of cats, dogs, and miscellaneous others were trapped and in difficult cases, tranquilized and transported out as soon as the weather allowed. Most survived, and many were reunited with their original families and treated for radiation poisoning. Cathy and Jill kept two of the cats, whose owners couldn't be found, and Chester the dog, because he needed extra care his original owners couldn't afford. Claude the pot-bellied pig had originally lived quite near the power plant, and he didn't make it.

Dreamy St. Maarten

I'm on the beach. It's dark. Someone's chasing me. I look over my shoulder and trip. The sand is soft where I fall. I scramble trying to stand. Too late. His knees hit my back, forcing the air from my lungs as he shoves my face into the sand. I flap, a fish on dry land. Sand fills my mouth, my throat. I lie still.

"Wakey, wakey, sunshine!" Ethan is pounding on the cabin door.

I struggle out of the tangled bed sheets; my head feels like an overripe melon looking for an excuse to burst. "Please, Ethan!" I whisper, trying not to trigger a cranial explosion. "Can't I have a lie in? It's my day off."

I don't think he heard me. He's already heading back to the cockpit. "We have to move the boat," he calls. "On deck. Chop, chop."

I stand on shaky legs, wrapping a sarong around me and fumbling for my sunglasses. Clothing may have been optional, but shades for my bleeding eyes, not so much.

Damn it. The floorboards rattle as the engine comes to life.

"Give me a minute!" I shout toward the cockpit on my way to the headache remedy in the galley cupboard. *Three tabs ought to do.* I chase them down with cold coffee and climb the companionway steps.

Everything's ready on deck. Ethan's at the helm. It's usually my job to pull the anchor, but he takes pity on me. "Look," he says, "You steer. I'll do the pulling today." He hops onto the deck, nimble as a cat, though I know he drank more than me last night. I'm happy to let him pull the stupid anchor. The owner of the clapped-out sailboat we run is too cheap to fix the windlass, and I'd spew for sure if I had to pull the anchor up by hand today. The last twenty feet of chain becomes absolutely nauseating.

It's flat calm, so we won't be putting up any sails. That's good. Ethan can motor around to the fuel dock, and I can go back to bed. That's the plan, but the diesel fumes turn my stomach as soon as I go below deck, and I heave my guts up. Through deep breaths, face to the porcelain, I wonder what I'm doing here. Ethan is a great guy—good skipper, funny, entertaining—but he can put away more drink than any single human I have ever known. When I go out with him, I get hangovers enough for both of us, but I go with him because I hate to think what he'd get into without any supervision.

Back in my bunk, I toss and turn, but I can't sleep. It's that dream. I pack it in after half an hour and go back to the cockpit.

"I thought you were going to catch another couple of hours' kip," Ethan says when I emerge from the companionway.

"Bad dream," I tell him. After several months crewing with him, I've grown used to his Kiwi turns of phrase. You have a kip (nap) when you're knackered (tired).

"Yeah? What about?"

"Someone was chasing me on the beach. I tripped and he caught me. Forced my face down in the sand and smothered me. It felt so real, I woke up with grit in my teeth."

"Bugger me. They say if you die in your dream, you die in real life."

"I think I just proved them wrong."

Ethan is good company over a beer, but we tread a fine line. He's my boss, and while we're pretty casual with each other, there's no fooling around. I knew the little French girl working charters with him, and when her husband turned up, Ethan found himself in need of a cook fast. Ethan has terrible luck with women. He's into these barely legal bits of fluff that giggle a lot. I can't understand how an intelligent guy can put up with that. Maybe it's because they don't answer back when he's being an ass? I don't have that problem.

I have no problem calling him out when he's acting like a jerk. I'm tall and he's not. That's one thing that doesn't lend chemistry to our relationship. But there was also this one night when I punched him for auctioning me off in a Front Street bar; that put paid to any relationship ideas between us. Ethan swore it was a joke, but the whole thing went sideways when a seven-foot-tall Dutch sailor got way too friendly. I doused the guy in beer and raised hell. The sailor got kicked out of the bar, but not before he said that Ethan charged him money for my services. It felt really satisfying to slug Ethan right there in front of God and everybody. Then I got him a cloth for his nose, helped him up, and we left together. He apologized in the dinghy all the way back out to the boat, and now the whole thing's just a funny story.

I'm glad of the job with Ethan even if he is full of it sometimes. Going to work aboard *Illusion* with him meant I could get off the day-sailing crews and give up my stinky apartment behind the Asian grocery. Besides, what's not to love about getting paid to take people to the most beautiful beaches in the world?

"More coffee?" I turn toward the galley. My head is throbbing again.

"Yes, please." Ethan holds his cup out for a refill.

I rummage around and come back with coffee and toast. "There's not much left. The Munich drinking team cleaned us out." Most times, charter guests will have a couple of meals ashore and give me a night off, but the German men we had just dropped off had taken every meal onboard. They went ashore just long enough for me to clean their smelly, horrible cabins. Ethan busted his tail, too, ferrying them around and keeping things above deck in order.

"They drank all the beer, too, the wankers," Ethan says.

"Still no tip money?"

"Not a sausage." He shakes his head and pulls on the cigarette that's beside him. Some charter guests are just like that. They work you to death and all you get is a handshake.

I say, "Bastards. Ask the broker to explain about the tip next time, would you?"

Ethan thinks that's funny. "I doubt it'll do any good," he says.

Still, working as a charter cook beats hell out of being a deckhand on a catamaran—my previous job. Those guys paid crap wages for me to tend to as many hungover tourists as they could fit on their wide, multi-hull decks. The only thing they asked when they hired me was "Do you get seasick?" And whoever had the grossest story at the end of the day earned a free beer at happy hour.

"So, what's the news?" I ask, pointing at Ethan's fresh newspaper.

"Some American bird's gone missing."

He flings the paper at me like a Frisbee, and I catch it awkwardly. The story is at the top of page one. I skim quickly: the girl was twenty-two, missing for three days, down here on her own, just graduated from college.

I think, *Dumbass. This is no place for a privileged American girl on her own.* Between the old expat lechers and the local boys, everybody thinks you're a slut. You don't have to do anything wrong. It's just the way things are. The easiest community for a girl on her own to break into is the yachtie community—if she has a strong stomach.

"She's probably dead," I say, looking at the picture her family has given to the press—blonde hair, blue eyes, perfect tan—just like Pamela Anderson on *Baywatch*.

"Yeah." Ethan sounds sad. She's his kind of girl.

This bitch is playing with me. Stupid cow! Dress that way. 'Course she gonna fall down. I'll teach that American whore to drink rum like a man.

"Hell-o-o. Take the wheel? I need a piss." The mizzen and the jib are flogging, and the boat is nose-up into the wind. A breeze has come up to port, and the water's turned to chop. Ethan has run up a little canvas fore and aft for stability, though he's still relying on the engine to push us forward.

"Huh? Oh, sorry. I fell asleep."

"I didn't like to wake you, but . . ." He gestures toward the useless autopilot.

How the hell did you get the sails up without me, I wonder, but I get up and take the wheel. We're still an hour from Phillipsburg.

"I was dreaming again. This time *I* was chasing some girl on the beach—like I'm in the guy's head this time. Got my adrenaline up. I feel kind of sick from it."

"Charming," Ethan says. "Probably from reading that story in the paper."

"He was so angry." I say, but I can't help feeling it was more than that. The feeling in my gut was visceral. I *wanted* to kill that American slut.

We motor along listening to music. As we pass the dump, I wonder what it must have been like before the locals pushed all the old cars off the cliff into the sea there. I used to know a guy on the cars. His wife dumped him, and one day he took a swim off this point and met with a shark. At least that's what everybody thinks happened to him. His body never turned up. There are sharks in the area, for sure. The slaughterhouses throw carcasses off the cliff here too.

At the fuel dock I ask Ethan, "So, what do you have planned for the rest of the day?"

"I'm going to wash the deck and topsides, and you are going to provision."

I find a driver I know at the taxi stand on Front Street. He's one of Everton's boys, and the magnetic "Everton Taxi" sign on the car door shows a yellow bird in a hat with a black and white checkered hatband.

"Irie." The young Rasta beams his hundred-watt smile at me. "How we be rollin' this fine morning, Miss?"

"Morning, Eustace," I say.

He shakes his locks and flips them over his shoulder like a fashion model sucking his teeth. "You must call I Tuff."

"Sorry, Tuff. I forgot. Can you run me to the market?" I know his older sister from the cats, and she introduced him as Eustace, so that's how I think of him.

"Irie, sista!" I get in and he slams the little car into gear, roaring out onto the main road—music turned up to eleven. What the car lacks in polish it makes up for in noise-generation.

I hold on tight and lean back. Third World belts out "Ninety-Six Degrees in the Shade"—one of my favorites— and I sing along. Tuff pulls a spliff out from behind his ear, raising his eyebrows at me. I nod. Three songs later we're outside the market, and my head feels a little better as Tuff roars off waving out the window and shouting "Rastafari!"

The market is a huge warehouse filled with the smell of rotten fish. *Why is the fish market the first thing you come to?* I wonder. I aim for the wine and booze—heavy stuff first. Then I wend my way through the acres of warehouse to finish with bread and flowers. I've filled three carts, and my purse is two-grand lighter. I plan to feed and entertain six people for a week with a little judicious planning and a fresh fish or two Ethan is sure to catch along the way.

Stepping out into the parking lot, the sunlight stabs my eyes before I can raise my sunglasses. A middle-aged driver with café-au-lait skin is waiting for a fare, and I wave. We load the groceries into his minivan. *It's a good thing Tuff isn't waiting for me,* I think. We never would have fit all the groceries in his little car, but I wish I could smoke another spliff. The West Indies is playing cricket against India, and the driver, Franklin, the license posted on his dashboard says, is absorbed in the radio coverage. I pull a paperback out of my bag, but I don't read a full sentence before the bright sun sends me to sleep.

I'm dancing. It's a jump-up in some little pavilion bar over by the lagoon. The music is way too loud. The place is packed. It's hard to push through the crowd. I'm going to vomit, and I stumble outside.

"Miss, Miss. We reach the marina." Franklin touches my shoulder.

"Oh," I mumble, wiping my face. "Was I snoring?" But the driver is out of the van and walking around to open the back door where half the groceries are stored. By the time I get out, he's got the side door open for me to start getting things out that way. Ethan meets me at the dock, and we haul everything to the boat in the dinghy. It takes us over an hour to run back and forth and stow everything, but eventually we head back in for beer and sandwiches at the bar.

"You look like shit," Ethan says when the waiter sets our beers down.

"Gee, thanks." I have no witty comebacks. "I can't wait to get away from this island. I haven't had a decent sleep since we got here."

"I thought it was the drink."

I shake my head. "Nope. Even sloshed I can't sleep. It's these awful dreams."

"Still?"

"Yeah. Every time I drift off."

"Same dream?"

"No, but they're connected. If I'm not running for my life, I'm trying to kill somebody."

* * *

It's still dark when we slip out of the harbor and head for Saint Vincent and the Grenadines. For two weeks, we sail and play with a family from Ohio. It's their first time on a sailboat, and they take Ethan's word as gospel—follow his every suggestion. We finish the charter on a high. Good group, good weather, good tip. No dreams. Everything's going great until the engine breaks down just south of St. Maarten.

We barely have the anchor set in Simpson Bay when the VHF crackles to life.

"*Illusion, Illusion, Illusion*, this is the *Molly B.*" Nils, my Scanderhooligan sometimes boyfriend, must have heard Ethan on the radio talking to the harbormaster about getting into the Lagoon to get a mechanic on the boat. Ethan likes to call himself "Mr. Bloody Fixit," but he knows when it's a job for a professional.

We just missed the last bridge opening for the day, so we're rocking and rolling in the bay. The bridge doesn't open again until 6:00 a.m., so we put out a stern anchor to keep the boat from dragging onto the rocks. We're dirty and tired, and ready to get off the boat for a while, especially since there's no hot water with the engine down.

"*Molly B., Molly B., Molly B.*, this is the *Illusion*," I sing into the radio. "Switch to 22." I turn the little knob on the top of the radio. "*Molly B., Molly B.*, this is *Illusion*. You copy?"

"*Illusion*, this is *Molly B.*," comes Nils' Norwegian accent. "Where are you?"

"Simpson Bay, wrong side of the bridge, over."

"Bad luck. We got through in time on the French side, over."

"We're heading in to shower at the marina."

"Bar de la Mer at seven-thirty?"

Nils has a wife back in Norway, but he says he'll never go back there. He would like me to settle down with him in a grass hut on the beach somewhere, but it doesn't feel right. We just take things day-by-day.

Ethan shares the taxi to Marigot and joins Nils and me for one drink, which turns into four drinks, and before we know it we're off on a drunken adventure! Nils and Ethan both refill my glass many times, and they get pretty wrecked too, because neither of them notices that I'm having trouble walking as we head out of Bar de la Mer. We get in a taxi and Nils gives the driver an address in Les Terres Basses where he's heard about a party. I put my head on his shoulder and close my eyes.

Whore of Babylon. Drinking like a man. Shame to see it. Teach the bitch a lesson.

Nils shakes me awake. It's dark. The taxi has stopped, and Ethan pulls me out through the side door.

"Where are we?" I ask.

"*Shhh.*" He moves to stand between the taxi and me.

Nils is the last one out, but instead of coming to stand by me and Ethan, he leans in through the passenger window and says something to the driver that I can't quite hear.

"Driver wants two hundred US to take us the rest of the way," Ethan whispers in my ear.

"Or what? He leaves us here?" I ask.

Ethan shrugs, and that's when Nils reaches through the window, grabs the driver by the collar, and drags him across the front seat and halfway out the passenger window. His right arm moves like a snake. It's the only time I have ever seen him do anything even remotely aggressive, though I know he used to box back in Norway.

Ethan lunges, wrapping his arms around Nils and lifting him off his feet to break his grip on the driver who is wedged head and shoulders in the window frame, blood dripping from his nose. The man wrenches himself back into the driver's seat, yanks down the gear lever, and spins the tires, spraying gravel at us as he leaves.

"I've got my handheld," Ethan says waving the radio around.

Nils fumes. I've never seen him like this, and I don't know what to say, so I leave him alone and stagger to a big rock where I sit and let my head spin.

"Everton Taxi, Everton Taxi, Everton Taxi, this is the *Illusion*," Ethan calls into the radio. He doesn't even slur.

Somebody mans Everton Taxi's base unit twenty-four seven, but it takes a while before a sleepy voice responds. "*Illusion*, this is Everton Taxi. Take it to twenty-two."

"Everton Taxi, this is *Illusion*. Do you copy?" Ethan repeats on the new channel.

"I copy, *Illusion*. Where you call from this morning?"

"We had some trouble. We're on the Sandy Ground road. West side of Nettle Bay," Ethan says.

I'm glad somebody knows where we are.

Eustace or rather Tuff shows up eventually and loads us into his little car. The back seat is cramped but clean. I sit there beside Nils, but I don't lean on him.

Tuff asks Ethan, "What happen, Cap?"

"Guy had a gun. He said if we didn't give him two hundred US, he'd leave us out here to walk."

Schtoops. "Me a warn you! Who this guy is?"

"I didn't get his name. Taxi driver with a minivan," Ethan says and shakes his head.

Tuff swings his dreads. "You want I take you to the police station?"

"We're pretty wrecked here. He didn't take anything. You think it's gonna do any good?"

"Mon, we got troubles on the island, Cap. Girls them missin'. You doesn't must, but maybe best you does."

"I marked him," Nils says. His voice is a low growl.

We all look at him.

Ethan laughs and nods. Tuff raises an eyebrow and looks at Nils in the rearview.

"Bastard said something about trading favors with Laura if we didn't pay," Nils says. It's news to me and Ethan. Neither of us had heard what set Nils off.

Ethan says, "Nils dragged the bastard through the passenger window and went to work."

Tuff shakes his head again. "Look like we hafta go to the police. Best you tell the story first. Sure, the taxi man gonna report something."

By three a.m. when I finally get to tell my version, I'm stiff and sore from sleeping on a bench in the waiting area of the *Gendarmerie.* I tell the French policeman what I remember then wait for Nils and Ethan. It's 4:45 when we finally pile into the dinghy.

The man is chasing me around rusty old cars—some on their sides, some upside down. I reach the shore and slip into the water. I hear him calling from up the hill. "Here kitty, kitty, kitty . . ." I am afraid to go too deep in the dark water, but I hear him coming closer . . .

It feels like there's gravel under my eyelids, and the boat's moving. I roll out of the bunk, grabbing clothes as I go thinking the anchor must be dragging. Then I remember Nils is with us. They've left me to sleep while they go through the drawbridge, Nils in the dinghy pulling us, Ethan at the helm. We're easing into a slip with the help of some other guy in a dinghy when I get to the cockpit.

"'Bout time, sleepy head. Grab some fenders," Ethan says.

As soon as we're situated, Ethan charges off to find a mechanic while Nils and I go back to bed.

The taxi man says, "You the guy I see with that missing girl? You gonna need some US dollars, my friend." I jerk him through the window. That damned little Kiwi bastard pulls me off before I can shut the guy up.

There's a knock on the hull, and I jerk awake. A voice with a Dutch accent calls, "Permission to come aboard."

I shout through the hatch, "Just a minute!" and climb over Nils to rummage through the heap of clothes on the floor. I run my fingers through my hair on the way to the cockpit. A tall man in starched khakis greets me from the dock, his badge reflecting light at me.

"Come aboard."

"Thank you," he says. He swings a long leg up over the guardrail.

"Coffee?" I ask.

"No thanks. I'm here to follow up on the report you made earlier this morning."

"You from the Dutch side?" I ask. "We were at the *Gendarmerie* in Marigot last night."

That's when Nils makes his way up the companionway. His shirt is wrong-side-out.

"I know you talked with the *gendarme* last night, but I'd like to hear your stories again, please. I'm working on a different case."

"The missing girl?"

"I'm not at liberty to say."

We tell our stories again. I don't mention my dreams.

*　*　*

Nils ships out on the Molly B. the following day, and while Ethan has the boat torn up so the mechanic can access the engine, I visit the Dutch detective one more time. And that's the last thing I do on St. Maarten, or Sint Marten either, for that matter.

We finish the season with back-to-back charters out of Antigua, and Ethan and I get good and drunk one last time. We're tied up at the dock in Falmouth Harbour, and I screw my sunglasses on tight as I tiptoe up on deck. Ethan has left his hatch open, and I can hear him snoring from the dock as I turn toward Nelson's Dockyard.

The taxi driver is an old man driving the early morning shift. We ride in silence to V. C. Bird International Airport. One-way ticket to Miami. Round trip would be cheaper, but I don't plan to come back this way again. Cheaper to make a stop in St. Maarten, but I pay the extra to avoid that airspace. I peal five one-hundred-dollar bills off my roll of tip money and pass them over to the sour-faced girl staring down her nose at me from the ticket counter.

Just short of sneering, her eyes run over my T-shirt, shorts, and flip-flops. She hands me my ticket. Her mouth says, "Have a nice flight," but her eyes say, "Fuck off and die."

Chumming for Sharks

Cash at the end of the day. That's all I was after. I knew I wouldn't be able to trade on my looks forever, but if my bikini helped me to land a job, so be it. Who was I to turn down work on a rich man's boat? I was winding up a varnishing job in a little marina just south of Ft. Lauderdale, and I'd gone up to the café for lunch when all hell broke loose.

It started with the big powerboat at the end of the T-dock suddenly going quiet—generators and everything. Next thing I knew people were yelling and running. The cops got there fast. You couldn't really see much from then on once the ambulance came to take away what was left of the poor guy. Somehow the sign the captain swears he hung on the ignition key in the wheelhouse wasn't there when the mate switched on the mains. You know, the one that says, "DIVER DOWN. DO NOT START MAIN ENGINE." He claims the captain radioed and told him to fire it up to test something and there wasn't any sign. The captain says *he* wasn't even there when it happened. He never called the mate, and there's nobody to corroborate his story. Poor guy. The cops hauled him off.

Pretty much everybody who'd been milling around trying to see what was going on headed to the café for a beer. It was only one o'clock, but the accident convinced us to give up on doing anything meaningful for the rest of the afternoon. It was our way of showing respect for the dead. I found myself seated next to a deep-sea fishing boat captain whose shirt had "Deep Sea Dan" embroidered over his left breast pocket. He had crinkly leather skin, a gold signet ring, and greasy hair slicked back.

"Haven't seen you here before," he said.

"I'm doing some varnishing up in the yard."

"That would explain the dust." He looked me over taking in the bandana around my head, the clear patches where my sunglasses had been, my bikini top and cut-off jeans—all of it covered in the fine yellow dust that clung to anyone stripping old varnish.

"Yeah, we're taking a sweet little Chris-Craft back to bare wood. She is going to be gorgeous."

"Oh right. On the hard. You pass it coming in from the parking lot."

"That's the one." I sipped my beer. "Any idea who that diver was?"

"Some Italian kid, Guarino? I can't remember. He's scraped barnacles off my boat's hull before." Dan took a pull from his beer then said, "So do you only do varnishing?"

"No, no. I do just about any kind of day-work. I'll be looking for another job next week. You need your boat washed? Bilges painted?"

"Well," said Deep Sea Dan, "I might. Do you have a card?"

"Yes sir!" I whipped out my business card. It said, "Olivia Cleans Boats" and my phone number.

That evening, back aboard *Gypsy,* my guy Talbot and I were just finishing dinner and he said, "So you gave this old geezer your card?" Tal's a tall skinny guy who used to do custom cabinetry, but he also used to run drugs from Colombia, and he got caught. He'd nearly finished ten years as a guest of the State of Florida—he only had six months of parole left to serve. Until that was up, he had to work at a licensed facility that paid peanuts.

"He wasn't that bad, and yeah. I got nothing for next week. One of us needs a job that pays something."

"Don't get sassy with me, girl. I worry about you. You never know who you're working for," Talbot said.

"Maybe, but it beats the hell out of me riding the bike all over Fort Lauderdale just to find a job every morning."

"At least get the guy's name. 'Deep Sea Dan' tells me nothing."

Captain Dan called me that Friday morning early.

"Olivia? This is Dan Johnson. You remember? From the *Lulabel?*"

"Deep Sea Dan?"

He chuckled. "That's right."

"Yes, Captain. How can I help you?"

"I wonder if you might be interested in going out on the boat today? My regular mate isn't available."

"What would you need me to do?"

"Helm and clean-up mostly. There's nothing to it. I handle the fishing lines. A hundred dollars for the day. It's just the owner going out today. He won't stay too long. He just likes to take a ride, catch a nice dolphin for dinner. How soon can you get here?"

The old man, Mr. Agnoli, was no trouble at all. He traveled with a fox terrier named Pookie. I kid you not, Pookie! I hardly spoke to the old guy. Dan showed me how to drive the boat once we cleared the cut. *Lulabel's* big twin diesels made her easy to handle. He went down and looked after the boss. He didn't just bait the hooks, he even landed the fish. The boss just sat smoking a cigar and enjoying the breeze. Dude wore horn-rimmed coke-bottle glasses tinted a shade of green I'd only ever seen on old men. Little bits of conversation drifted up to me in the tuna tower. It sounded like they were speaking Italian. When we got back to the dock, Dan showed me how he liked the fish filleted. Then I washed the boat down and went home.

We rocked along like that with Dan calling two or three days a week, and it was almost always the boss. Sometimes with and sometimes without his wife. The only thing that came up was when the missus, Lucile, the *Lu* in *Lulabel*, with daughters Laura and Isabella accounting for the *La* and the *Bel*, told Dan that I was to keep my blouse buttoned up at all times. Guess the old man had commented on my bikini top. It irked me, but I respected the old girl's wishes. From then on I wore khakis, boat shoes, and a buttoned white blouse. I'd only ever strip down to the bathing suit once everybody had gone so I could clean fish and wash down.

Dan would go off to the bar with them and leave me to put the boat to bed. He came back one evening as I was finishing up and pulled the creeper routine on me, though. Grossed me right out. When I told Talbot about it, he acted like he was gonna go confront Captain Dan.

"Man! I don't trust that guy." He stomped around on deck grumbling.

"He's harmless. Probably can't even get it up," I said.

"You don't find many Italians named Johnson. I bet that's not even his real name."

"Tal, what is your problem? It's easy work, and I'm making the money for two weeks' worth of groceries in a day. Who cares if the dude doesn't use his real name?"

Not long after that we took the Desideris out. Captain Dan called later than he usually did. I was already on the bike asking around at the small marinas on 17th Street.

"Can you go fishing today? I got a last-minute charter. There's some tip money in it."

Turns out it was a guy named Desideri and his son. The son's name was Rick, and he might have been twenty. It was hard to tell. He could have been younger. Dan gave the dad a funny look when they arrived—and the guy smiled and said something I didn't quite catch, but it put Dan in a bad mood for the whole trip. Never took his eyes off those two. He sent me up the tuna tower immediately—even let me take her out through Port Everglades—like he didn't trust our guests alone on deck. He came up to spell me for a few minutes about mid-morning and saw I was sweating.

"The boss's wife isn't here. You can peel down to the swimsuit if you want. Might add to the tips."

The Desideris wanted to go shark fishing, and Dan had just poured out the bloody, smelly mess he mixed up to chum for sharks when a huge tiger shark struck. The kid fought for three solid hours. Nobody spelled him. Pissed me off when his dad shot the shark. Dan kept a shotgun propped up on the stern for emergencies, but this guy pulled his own handgun. It was Florida, after all, so I didn't think much about the fact that he'd brought a handgun. I just figured they'd cut the shark loose. That's what Dan usually did with sharks. Instead, we dragged her, all twelve feet of her, to the dock for pictures. Dan used my phone to take the pictures since his old-school camera used film, and the Desideris wanted pics they could share right away.

Desideri didn't even want the meat. Just the jaws. Dan didn't want the meat either, so Talbot came and butchered the carcass. We still have shark meat in our freezer.

The Desideri boys were gone when Tal got there. He'd had to dinghy all the way around from Lake Sylvia where *Gypsy* was anchored. It was faster on the bike, but we needed a way to get all that meat home. It was still light out, but not for long. Bottom line is he didn't get a look at Tommy Desideri until I showed him the pictures we took with the shark that afternoon. He snatched the phone out of my hand.

"What did you say this guy's name was?"

"Desideri."

"Tommy?"

"Maybe. The kid's name is Rick."

"Do you know who Tommy Desideri is?"

"No, should I?"

"He's a hitman, Olivia. Big time." Tal was staring daggers at me.

"Seriously?" I thought about it a minute. "He did have a gun. And Dan sure gave him the hairy eyeball. Kind of acted like a jerk all day."

"He was probably scared shitless. I guarantee you Dan knew who this guy was. He must have connections working for Agnoli and all."

Tal had already dredged up an old article that showed Mr. Agnoli walking out of a New York courtroom when he was younger. Apparently the old guy had retired from the life, but he still knew people.

"Okay, but Desideri's kid was with him. I'm sure he was just there to fish. Mr. Agnoli probably owed him a favor or something."

"A favor, yeah. Baby, I don't want you working for these people anymore. They carry guns. What if Desideri's visit wasn't innocent? These guys don't leave witnesses."

Once again, I didn't take Tal's advice. Dan wanted me to come clean the boat. What could be the harm in that? I went down there.

Dan was organizing his tackle, and, like an idiot, I said, "Can you believe Talbot thought Mr. Desideri was a hitman?"

"Did he? Wonder what gave him that idea?" Dan didn't look up.

"I don't know. He's from New Jersey, you know?"

I finished my work. Then on the way up the dock to the ATM machine Dan says, "I've enjoyed having you work with me, Liv." He gave me a weird little sideways nod.

I caught this expression on his face for just a second out of the corner of my eye. It was, I don't know, regretful? I didn't know what to say. It sounded like he was firing me.

Then as we passed by the stern of this big gin palace reversing into a slip, Dan shoved me, hard, into the water. I didn't have time to think, and it was just luck that stopped me choking. If I'd done anything but what I did, which was to get low down in the mud and swim under the boats, he'd have seen me. I had to be in shock, because I felt calm.

I peeked through the slats of the dock and saw Dan about three slips away looking for me in the water. He had a gun in his hand. He didn't see me, so I ducked back down. I'm a strong swimmer, and I swam to the fuel dock. The trick was getting out of the water without being seen. I raised up and saw Dan walking slowly the other way up the dock we'd been on, and I rolled into a random dinghy and prayed the owner of the thing wouldn't raise the alarm as I headed for *Gypsy*.

"You said what?" Talbot shouted at me. He had both hands on my shoulders.

"I told him what you said about Tommy Desideri." I clenched my teeth to keep them from chattering. "I'm a blabbermouth." I half expected Talbot to smack me—he looked so angry—but he let out a growl and hugged me instead.

"So, he tried to push you into a running prop?"

"Yeah."

"And you saw him with a gun in his hand?"

"Yeah."

He let me go and his voice got serious. "We have to move the boat. Now."

We were almost through the cut when I heard Captain Dan on the radio.

"Port Everglades Pilot. . . . Port Everglades Pilot. . . . This is *Lulabel*, Whiskey Yankee Papa sixteen twenty-nine."

"Oh my God, Tal! That's him."

"I hear. Get the binoculars. See if you can see him. We need to disappear."

I couldn't see *Lulabel*, but I knew *Gypsy*'d never outrun her if Dan saw us. I gave up looking and hopped back into the cockpit.

"What are we going to do now?" I know I must have looked desperate. I was still shaking.

"We're going to outsmart him. Get the main up. We'll hide among the other sailboats. It'll be a good downwind run to the Keys."

That's when I remembered Rick Desideri's number was still in my phone. I had texted the shark pictures to him. Thank God for waterproof cases, I thought.

We tucked Gypsy into a little hurricane hole Tal knew about. It was in the mangroves north of Key Largo. A deep canal had been dredged so sailboats could shelter there in rough weather. At least that's what Tal said he'd used it for. I figured he knew it from his drug running days. Right now, that didn't matter. We were hidden—just not very well—especially if you were up on the US 1 Bridge.

It was late afternoon when we heard big engines slow to an idle near the entrance of the canal. We figured Dan would be hunting *Gypsy*'s mast poking up above the mangroves, so we were in the dinghy hidden back among the mosquitos in the swamp.

I saw Dan start down the ladder from the tower, and then . . . his head exploded.

I nearly screamed but stopped myself. I swung the binoculars up to look at the bridge, where I knew the Desideris had waited, feigning a flat tire.

I could just imagine the father clapping his son on the shoulder. He'd say, "Good shooting, boy." And I could feel the gunsight following me. *Please God don't let them shoot me.* My jaw trembled so I couldn't have spoken if I tried, but I prayed very loud in my head. The imaginary hitman in my head said to his son, "You give out your phone number to a girl again and I'll pop you myself."

"Here we go," Talbot hissed, snapping me out of my imagination. He took a breath and gunned the outboard. "Stay low."

A Simple Twist of Fate

She grabbed the doorknob, but it wouldn't turn. Justine let out a sort of groaning howl but resisted the urge to bang on the metal siding of the port-a-can. The men's door was ajar, and she sucked in a deep breath before going in. Her eyes watered from the smell, though she continued to hold her breath and raced to get her belt unbuckled and her pants down before she soiled herself. At least she hadn't worn the heavy velvet skirts she'd originally planned to wear, opting instead for simple black jeans and a T-shirt so she could move freely under her cloak—the real centerpiece of the outfit she'd spent months embroidering. She'd wear the velvets in daylight later in the fair.

"Might be a touch of IBS," the doctor had said, but apparently, he knew no remedy for it. Justine would just have to carry on shitting her guts out. She should have had a colonoscopy before she quit her job, but she hadn't thought that far ahead. She hated to admit it, but her mother had been right with her doom and gloom prognostication about how Justine would regret leaving a good job with health insurance. Working freelance had proven to be a double-edged sword. She'd stopped being embarrassed about her frequent, explosive trips to the toilet, and the occasional "accident" that required a change of clothes had become much easier to deal with, but she'd lost her health insurance, and couldn't afford to track down the underlying cause of her gastric distress. She'd grown complacent working from home, otherwise, she'd have taken precautions and not found herself in this dreadful situation in a port-a-can at the Renaissance Faire's After Hours Fête.

She and her friend Sheila had been planning this evening for months. Sheila, because it was a great party populated by handsome, unattached men, and Justine, to show off her beautiful costumes. Romance was the farthest thing from Justine's mind, but she had slaved over Sheila's dress—a historically accurate French court dress with elaborate gold brocade panels in a rich blue satin. Sheila was the only friend Justine had made at her old job, even though she'd worked there for five years. She'd never been "one of the girls," and when the IBS started, the gossips in accounting she had to waddle past on every single trip to and from the toilet had gotten ugly. First, they'd made up a name tag and stuck it on the last stall door—indicating that they didn't want to share the same shitty seat with her. Potpourri and spray deodorizer had materialized next to the toilet over the course of a few weeks with cutesy little PSAs taped to the inside of the door about the importance of handwashing, and that whole group of cookie-cutter women with their I-want-to-speak-to-the-manager haircuts stopped making eye contact with her after a particularly messy day when she had to leave early. She'd agonized about quitting that job, though she'd been doing graphic design work freelance on the side for a while.

She and Sheila had bonded over the Ren Faire when Justine had brought her sword to work one day and explained that she fenced in a gym after work. Sheila, a brash blonde beauty who worked in sales, had badgered Justine until she'd finally invited her to go to the gym with her, and then to the Ren Faire later that year. Sheila had drooled over the men fencing at the gym, but wasn't much into getting sweaty herself, but she loved dressing up and turning heads. The

Renaissance Faire had become an annual event for the two of them with the pair attending every weekend through the six weeks the fair was open. The opening night fête was always a big deal.

Justine, for her part, loved everything about the Renaissance period, and if there were a time machine, she'd be first in line to go back. Before the IBS stuff, she'd fenced two or three times a week, but that had become problematic when the unpredictable bouts of diarrhea started, so now, she focused on the clothes. She'd spent many a night embroidering a sleeve or engineering some unique, but anachronistically correct fastener. And as with all art, her handiwork was only really valid if it had an audience. So, the annual Ren Faire was an event not to be missed.

She'd ignored the gastritis signals as she buckled her sword on that evening. *Why didn't I take anything for it?* she wondered. She flipped up the plastic cover over the toilet roll, and *THERE ISN'T ANY PAPER! Oh, God!* What was she supposed to do in this nasty, horrible little plastic bathroom with no running water? There was a tiny sink outside the cubicle with a foot pump to allow minimal handwashing, but to actually clean her behind, she'd have to waddle out there with her pants around her knees and wash herself for all to see with water that couldn't possibly be sanitary. *This has to be some sort of health violation*, she thought. Shouldn't there be a minimal amount of toilet paper required per person at an event? She guessed that this bank of potties had seen a disproportionate amount of traffic.

Squatting above the seat so as not to touch it, she rummaged clumsily in the historically accurate draw-string purse that hung from her belt. She held her pants, sword clattering awkwardly, with one hand attempting to keep them out of the puddle on the floor as her one and only lipstick splashed into it. "Shit," she said. It had been the perfect shade to enhance her full lips without looking unnatural. She was relieved, finally, to discover a crumpled grocery receipt with which she did her best to clean her backside. Up to that point she was coping. It was when she stood to pull her pants up that the real disaster struck. Her brand-new phone flipped out of her pocket into the fetid blue water of the porta-a-potty.

The people in line outside the port-a-potties thought maybe a crime had been committed when they heard the howl from behind the men's door. That is, until Justine emerged, wild-eyed, and wailed, "I've dropped my phone in the blue water!"

The first guy in line was obviously meant to be some sort of merchant with a long gray beard, brown breeches and hose, and an embroidered brown waistcoat over a puffy-sleeved shirt—also brown. Peasant but not. The handwork was too fine. A gold ring sparkled in one ear. "M-huh-lady," he spluttered and guffawed, bowing.

Justine scowled at the man and said, "It's not funny! My phone is in the port-a-potty!"

"Ah, love. I think you'll be needing a new phone."

The guy behind him pushed past and into the open door muttering, "Some of us still have to take a leak."

Justine whipped around as the door snicked closed. "No! Don't pee on my phone!"

At that, the brown man, well in his cups, doubled over. He was holding himself now so he wouldn't wet his pants. "You-hou-hou are killing me-he-he-he! *Don't pee on her phone!*"

Justine went down the three steps to ground level where her boot crunched in the gravel that lined the entire tent complex. She looked around for an attendant or anyone else who worked there. She wondered how long it would take the nasty blue chemicals to entirely consume her phone. She couldn't afford a new one. *Can it even be repaired if they get it out of there?* she wondered. Nirvana's "Smells Like Teen Spirit" whined from speakers on the tentpoles. It was deafening, which made it hard to have any sort of conversation. A steady stream of revelers flowed through the tents, stopping at buffet tables along the way and taking turns blocking the flow of the gravel-crunching crowd as conversations sprung up in the middle of the path. Pulsating purple, blue, and pink strobe lights made it hard to recognize the waiters, especially with everyone in Renaissance garb. People in voluminous costumes were rocking out along the way, and four geometric shapes suspended from chain at the corners of the dancefloor in the twenty-foot-high main tent held scantily clad nymphs and satyrs dancing seductively.

At that moment, however, the festive air was lost on Justine as she focused on getting to somebody, anybody who could help her get her phone out of the port-a-potty She finally reached the bar, just as Kurt Cobain reached a crescendo, screaming "a denial, a denial, a denial." Justine spotted a wench with breasts bulging out of her loosely cinched blouse, recognizable as staff only by the drink tray she held. Justine pressed as close as she was able, and yelled into the woman's ear, "My phone fell in the port-a-potty." Of course, that's right when the song finished and everybody around her heard. One guy spit his drink on his date as he burst out laughing.

The waitress turned to the bartender. "Ruthie! Clean-up in the port-a-potties." She turned back to Justine. "There's a guy with a swimming pool net somewhere around here." She chuckled. "Sorry."

Justine stood there, unclear what to do next, and waited for the guy with the net, *one drink and a puff on the hookah pipe is all I'm going to get out of this very expensive party*. She'd been so happy for a chance to show off her beautiful cloak, and she wasn't even wearing it. She was as embarrassed to be standing here out of costume as she was about her predicament with the phone. At least her beautiful cloak had survived the port-a-potty debacle. Sheila had it over at the hookah table. Beautiful costumes swirled around her, but she could hardly take them in. A juggler with flaming red hair and a bright green tartan kilt paused by her and wiggled his eyebrows suggestively as he threw a club over his shoulder and caught it. He moved on once he'd made her smile. The bartender tapped her on the shoulder and said, "I'm sorry, but you're blocking my run rail. The waiters need to get up here. Where are you hanging out? We'll come find you."

"The hookah tables." Justine said and pointed to the area at the back of an adjoining tent. She guessed that she'd better go break the news to Sheila that they'd have to leave early.

She made her way to Sheila and shouted into her cloud of hair. "I've got the runs, and there's no toilet paper here."

Sheila turned to face her and shouted, "And?"

"I have to go home."

"Pull the other one," Sheila said, but in the space of about three seconds, her eyes flashed several clear, nonverbal messages: *do you know what I paid for these tickets?* and *we just got here* and *call a fucking Uber.*

Attempting to soften the blow, Justine said, "Hang out for a little longer. I also dropped my phone in the port-a-can."

Sheila blew a lungful of smoke out, coughing. "I can't take you anywhere! Look, look. Maybe they have some Imodium or something in the first-aid tent. Then let's see if there is any Uber service out here. I am *not* leaving this party yet." She scanned the area for a waiter, then, as she blew nearly perfect smoke rings, she shouted, "Can't you just hold it?"

With her eyes, Justine said *FUCK NO.* With her mouth, she said, "Where's the first aid tent?"

Sheila clearly wasn't going anywhere for the rest of the night. If things had gone to plan, Justine would have been the designated driver, but she knew Sheila would rather have the handsome knight beside her take her home, though that guy was currently telling a joke to the minstrel beside him. *Poor Sheila,* Justine thought. *Your gaydar is faulty, love.*

Sheila spotted a waiter, empty drink tray held aloft. "Hey, waiter . . . where's the first-aid tent?" she shouted. Sheila's voice wasn't her best feature, and it came out sounding like a fishwife. The guy pointed, and Justine stood to head in that direction. Sheila yelled, "Take your cloak!" Then she made a telephone of her thumb and pinkie finger but giggled and shrugged when she remembered that Justine's phone was in the port-a-can.

The entrance to the first-aid tent was decorated with flower garlands and a sign that said, "Wise Woman in Residence." Inside, the tent looked like a school nurse's office with a paper-covered examination table, a desk, and a bored-looking woman in Cinderella scrubs filing her nails. Justine blinked in the bright white light and said, "Do you have anything for diarrhea?"

The nurse said, "I have. What seems to be the trouble?"

"It's IBS. I should have taken something before I left home."

"That's alright then. You sound sober. You haven't taken any drugs at all, have you?"

Justine shook her head *no*.

"I have to be careful what I administer to drunks. All part of the fun and games around here. I have some papers you have to sign. If you keel over, it's on you."

Next, Justine checked in with the bartender to see if her phone had been retrieved yet, but when her stomach began to gurgle, she turned toward the nearest bank of port-a-cans—two tents away. As she whirled around to face that direction, the same flame-haired juggler from earlier, leapt backward collecting his brightly colored balls as they fell from the air around her.

"Milady. I crave thy forgiveness." He bowed and his kilt flared around him. His long ginger hair was tied back with a strip of leather, and he was near enough that Justine could smell the peppermint soap he used.

Over the speakers, Dave Grohl belted out "What if I say I'm not like the others . . ."

Justine gave the juggler a faint, close-lipped smile, though the flutter in her chest was insistent enough that it momentarily overshadowed her urge to poop. She reined the irrational emotion aside. She'd seen his sort before—roving court jesters employed by the Faire. Apparently, this guy had been following her—making fun of her behind her back for the general amusement of other passersby. She hadn't noticed, but the people around her had. She saw a courtier duck his head in an attempt to hide his snickering. Her gut cramped and she grabbed her stomach and grimaced.

"Milady! Art thee unwell?" And just like that, the jester became a security guard.

"I need the toilet," Justine ground out.

"Take my arm, lady." The man, remaining in character, proffered his elbow.

Justine allowed the flamboyant character to pull her through the crowd to the staff toilets, hidden behind the bar by a wall of curtains.

"In here, lady."

Justine slipped out of her cloak, which she slung over the back of a convenient chair. "Can I leave this with you?" She barely registered the man's nod as she hurried into one of the staff toilets where she found ample toilet paper and a proper sink with running water. She emerged feeling much better and found the juggler standing at parade rest and guarding her cloak. "Thank you," she said.

"My pleasure, lady." He helped her back on with her cloak, then dropped the accent. "Pardon me asking, but are you the same lady who dropped her phone in the bog earlier?"

"Oh, yes!"

He pulled a small radio from his sporran, "Brian, I've found the lady who lost her phone. We're by the staff toilets." A garbled response followed, and ginger-man said to Justine, "He'll be along shortly. You know the phone is probably dead."

"Yes, but I need the corpse of the thing to take back to the place I bought it. I've only had it a week."

"Isn't that just the way. I'm Gerald."

"Justine."

A giant in simulated bear hide sauntered up and produced a Ziploc from some mystery pocket. Even in the oddly shifting colored light, Justine could see that the phone inside the bag was covered in unnaturally blue syrup. She reached out and pinched the bag between thumb and index finger. "Ewww, thanks," she said.

The giant smiled and shrugged. "Happens all the time."

"Are you the cell phone retriever, then?"

"Brian the giant, lady." He made little air quotes with his fingers when he said, "the giant."

"Justine. And really, I'm so embarrassed to put you to that trouble." She made to rummage in her purse for a tip.

Brian shook his head and indicated that he wanted no tip. His radio made a noise, from one of those secret pockets of his, and he rummaged around, eventually producing the device and turned aside to respond.

Overhead, Sublime sang about Santeria, and the nymphs and satyrs on their metal frames stretched into bizarre, contorted poses.

When Brian turned back, he took Justine's hand and said, "Lady, I must away. I pledge you my service. If ever you need me, you have but to ask." He kissed her hand and disappeared in three long strides.

Justine faced Gerald and offered him a little smile. "And thank you, Gerald."

"May I call someone for you? Your date?"

"Oh. Yes! I need a taxi or an Uber. My friend drove, but she isn't ready to leave."

"That'll be difficult. They don't come all the way out here. But the good news is that if you can wait half an hour, I'll do my act, and my shift will finish. I'd be happy to drive you. Wait back here if you like."

She thought about protesting, but she didn't since she saw no other way to get home. She said, "No, I'd like to see your act."

"Wonderful!" Gerald clapped his hands. "You can help!" And just like that, he leapt back into character. He grabbed Justine's hand and set off toward the main stage at a trot. As they approached the crowd around the stage, he said, "Make your way to about the third row back on the left side." He pointed.

Justine gulped.

"Your pardon, lady." He bowed and trotted off into the crowd leaving her to make her way into position.

The show was part juggling, part fire-eating, and part sleight-of-hand magic. About halfway through, Gerald pulled Justine from the audience "at random." She elbowed her way up to the stage where she stood like a deer in the headlights. Gerald was a pro and gave clear, if humorous directions that required little thought from Justine. She was as surprised as everyone else when the white bunny appeared from the hood of her cloak. While there was a collective "Awwww" from the audience at the rabbit's appearance, the real laugh came as Gerald grimaced and turned the cloak's voluminous hood inside-out dumping a handful of what appeared to be rabbit pellets on the floor. The audience was delighted.

Justine thought back to Gerald guarding her cloak. *The sly devil!*

Gerald winked at her.

Justine grinned, enjoying the laughter of the audience. All was well until Justine tripped on her cloak which caused Gerald to blow fire onto a barbarian in bear hide on the edge of the crowd. Justine held her hand to her eyes and recognized Brian the giant as he roared and charged the stage with a battle axe raised menacingly.

Gerald shouted, "Hide, lady!" and pointed to a large chest she could duck behind as he ran from one side of the stage to the other, barely outpacing the giant. As they drew near Justine's hiding place, instinct took over, and she leapt out with her sword performing a circular move to disarm the giant as she'd done a million times in the gym. The crowd went wild, and both Brian and Gerald bowed to her, then raised her arms high so she could take a bow with them and close the show.

When the lights went down, the two men laughed and clapped her on the back.

"What was that?" Brian asked.

"You are full of surprises, lady," Gerald said.

"I'm so sorry about tripping and making Gerald blow fire at you, Brian. Are you alright?"

"It was all part of the act, lady," Brian said.

"I tripped you," added Gerald.

"You should apply for a job. We could use you in the act," Brian said.

Justine thought for barely a heartbeat. "Do they offer health insurance?"

The Cistern

Each of the hotel's buildings, like all the converted structures on the island, sat above an enormous cistern that collected rainwater. The filtration systems were rudimentary with wire mesh screens to catch the largest particulates that might get into the water supply. We're talking about dead frogs and very large leaves. Smaller things got through, and if they were alive, they died in the dark water of the cistern and sank to the bottom.

When you first go to the islands that dot the Caribbean, you don't really think about where the fresh water comes from, and tourists use a lot of fresh water. It's an infrastructure nightmare. Those little independent nations down there have difficulty dealing with infrastructure sometimes. Once, for example, after the Canadian government gave our little island a huge new generator, the locals forgot to check the oil and burned the thing up in a matter of months. With regard to water, the digging of wells is strictly controlled by the government. You can't just go out and dig yourself a well, and there is no system of water mains.

Meanwhile, the tourists at the converted sugar plantation hotels leave the tap running while they brush their teeth and shower three times a day. So, where does all that fresh water come from? Rainwater. The hotels collect rainwater in cisterns under the buildings.

Most of the hotels on the island began as colonial-era sugar plantations, but this one was special—it had been a slave breeding farm. Guest rooms now filled the four-hundred-year-old buildings while the ghosts of laboring women wailed over the heads of the dancers on the nights when the rum punch flowed, and the steel band played.

The hotelier, my ex, called me one day in the off-season begging for my help. No water was flowing in one of his buildings, and he was too damned fat to get the pump out of the cistern to repair it, but he knew I had a mask and snorkel and an ego that wouldn't let me turn down an opportunity to show off my diving skills. He'd talked me into moving down there because he thought I had money. That was a joke. When he realized I wasn't an heiress with the funds to prop up his business, he had cast me aside. My pride wouldn't let me just leave and go home. I couldn't admit to the folks back home that my amazing Caribbean life was a sham, so I stayed, drinking too much and talking bad about Asshole the hotelier at every opportunity—especially to his guests. It made him furious to have to serve me in his bar, but if there was nobody else around, he'd still stop by my place for a quickie.

"No! I. Don't. Think. So." I pronounced each word clearly. "There are probably snakes and all sorts in there."

"They're not poisonous."

"Ewww . . . No. It'll be dark, and I know nothing about pumps or plumbing. What if I get electrocuted?"

"The power will be switched off."

"And you want me to fix this pump in the dark—underwater?"

"I'll be shining a light into the water the whole time. We can tie a rope around your waist in case you need to be pulled out. You just have to unplug the thing and bring it to me."

In spite of our messed-up relationship, I didn't believe he'd let me drown. Eventually, I agreed, and found myself easing my body into the scariest looking black hole I had ever seen. It was darker than I expected, and fucking freezing. The hatch was barely wide enough to allow my shoulders through.

Asshole held his big light.

I made a lot of noise about the cold, imagining some monster grabbing me from the darkness and pulling me down. Nobody came to see what the noise was about. Asshole had let the staff go for the summer. When I was halfway in, I decided to let go and drop all the way into the ice water. A wetsuit would have helped, but we hadn't thought of that. It was summer, after all.

Asshole aimed his light at the far corner of the cistern where the pump sat in a thick layer of rust-colored scum at the bottom of the very full fourteen-foot-deep cistern. I saw leaves, and hints of what looked like a frog carcass swirling in the muck. Enormous 12 x 12 hardwood beams supported the building above, and the still black water was touching the base of those beams and then some, I have no idea how many beams there are, but there was only about eight inches of air space at the top.

I strapped on a weight belt and slipped my fins on as I clung to the three-hundred-year-old wrought iron steps set into the wall, then gulped a giant breath and dove for that far corner. Asshole had told me I just had to unplug the thing and bring it up. I remember thinking, "Son of a bitch can get somebody else to put it back."

Disconnecting the pump proved to be the easy part, but I was gasping when I surfaced with it. With the weight belt on, it was a struggle to keep my face in the airspace above, but I didn't want to drop it. I'd never get it back, because I damn sure wasn't getting back in this water to get it out. I inhaled in ragged gasps, kicking hard and turning in circles. I couldn't find the hatch. The light was gone, and the airspace was dark. No handholds. *Shit, shit, shit!* The pump pulled at my left arm, but some stupid idea in my head made it important that I prove my physical prowess by completing my task, so I held onto it.

Kick. Kick. Kick. I swam awkwardly from one side to the other of the cistern, dragging the pump in one hand and feeling my way along the overhead beam with the other. Where was Asshole? What happened to the light? *I'm going to die right here in this cistern,* I thought, but that is when I looked down and saw a rusty orange glow, weak now because the bottom-slime had been stirred up by my fins. It dawned on me that the reason I'd lost sight of the entry hatch was because those support beams were blocking my view. My heart hammered in my chest, and I really wanted to pee in the cistern, but I held it out of some misplaced compassion for the tourists who would be bathing and brushing their teeth with this water in a few months. I sucked in a deep breath and ducked down under the support beam.

I was panting when I surfaced beneath the hatch and handed Asshole his pump. "Don't . . . ever ask . . . me to do that again."

He said, "Oh, I won't," right before he kicked me in the face, switched off his light, and replaced the hatch cover.

I'm learning to whistle between the buildings on the nights when the steel band plays.

Do You Know the Bunny Hop?

Elbert heard her coming, her tiny high-heeled shoes clipping along the pavement like a metronome. She approached his hotdog stand and said, "Blue moon, gesturing out loud," her voice rising at the end to make it a question.

He replied, "I had a pure-bred Schnauzer but now he only has three legs," and handed her a sweating bottle of water.

This wasn't the first time they'd played the word salad game. No telling what she meant to say, Elbert thought. She handed him a dollar and a quarter. As Mrs. Greenblatt turned away, he looked toward the next woman in line who was trying not to let on that she'd been listening, but puzzled amusement was plain on her face.

Elbert mouthed, "We're friends."

It was the same every day. Lois Greenblatt appeared like clockwork, a carefully coiffed, tissue-skinned creature barely tall enough to see above the top of his cart.

Water bottle in hand, Mrs. G., leaned down to the ancient coin-operated stand that held *The Chronicle* and read the headline. She gasped and brought a delicate hand up to her mouth. "Scented olive groves!" she muttered, shaking her head. Then straightening, she turned and walked away.

When she'd clicked back into the building, Elbert read the headline, "Robot Kills Gunman." He guessed it was the picture that had given her the meaning. Damage to her brain meant that words, spoken or written, no longer related to meaning for her. It must be hell, he thought, not to be able to say what you wanted.

Six weeks earlier, a small bespectacled man had approached as Elbert was shutting down for the day. "My mother has a condition known as Aphasia. Thank you for playing along earlier."

"Hmmm?" Elbert had looked up from the refrigerated compartment of the cart.

"My mother, the lady who came up speaking nonsense earlier?"

"Oh, yeah. Man, I'm sorry I barked at her like that. I didn't know she was . . . you know."

"No, no," the small man said. "She isn't crazy. It's a stroke, you see? She can't say the words she means to say. I just wanted to thank you for being polite and letting her work through it. Some people aren't as patient with her, but she still likes to get out—gives her a feeling of independence."

Elbert remembered she'd asked if he knew how to do the bunny hop, and he'd said, "Why, yes ma'am." He stuck his left foot out, then his right foot out, then hop, hop, hopped around in a tight little circle behind his wagon. His sense of fun was what brought the regulars back.

Mrs. G.'s brow had furrowed, and she said, "Nobel prize?"

Elbert tried a couple of times to get the woman to place her order. "Ma'am, I can't just be bunny hopping all day. Do you want something or not?" She hadn't understood him. "Did you want a dog?" He spoke louder, raised his eyebrows and waved a bun around in the air between them.

"Blue b-b-butter girl." Mrs. G. gave him a puzzled look as if he were the one speaking gibberish. She shook her head and frowned. Taking a deep breath, she pointed toward the water cooler.

When he handed her a water bottle, she smiled and paid him. He'd felt like a jerk all day for raising his voice to her, but she came back the next day and asked for "a slender cellist's chair" and he took in the faint whiff of moth balls around her, saw her bird-bright eyes. Elbert got used to seeing Mrs. Greenblatt, and when she missed a day, he wondered if she was okay. Occasionally the son scuttled by and waved, but he never stopped.

It had been Elbert who called the paramedics the Friday the skateboarding youth knocked Mrs. Greenblatt over and broke her hip. Elbert dialed 911 on his way to her, where she lay moaning on the sidewalk. He eased her head and shoulders off the hot pavement and sat down beside her. He hummed softly and held her at an angle that seemed to ease her pain while they waited for the ambulance. The son had ridden to the hospital with his mother. He hadn't thought to send word about her condition, and Elbert didn't see either of the Greenblatts at all the following week.

Finally, two weeks after the incident, Mr. Greenblatt came to the hot dog stand and offered Elbert a crisp hundred-dollar bill.

Elbert muttered and shook his head. "Naw, man, keep your money. Anybody would do the same."

"No, I don't think they would. You have no idea how much your little exchanges meant to her. She always enjoyed coming down to get her bottle of water from you."

"You say that like she won't be back."

"It doesn't look good. She's out of her mind since the surgery. Completely incommunicado. Doesn't know any of us, and honestly, I don't know how we'd know if she did."

Out of his cap and apron and wearing Sunday shoes, Elbert carried a small tropical plant he picked up at Walmart. He had to fight not to turn away from the pitiful sack of bones in the bed. But then she smiled, and he leaned in close.

Her voice was almost inaudible, but he clearly heard her say, "Do you know the bunny hop?"

Shit Happens

When it happened, it happened fast. We were scream-ing along on a downwind run with the spinnaker pulling us into a glorious South Pacific sunset. The boss and his guests stood toasting one another with champagne in crystal glasses. I'd tried to break him of that habit, because I was the one who ended up scrambling around after broken glass when someone forgot he'd set a glass down, and a jibe sent that glass flying. This time, though, the weather couldn't have been more perfect. I saw no danger in the champagne flutes. I'd topped them up and stood with Bill at the wheel.

None of us knew what happened. We were suddenly flying as the boat pitch poled and headed down. I caught the boss's eye as his glasses came unseated and his champagne glass left his hand in slow motion. His mouth was open, but I couldn't hear his voice with my own scream filling my ears. When the old man hit the water, I saw the boom smack the back of his head. His friends—who'd been forward of the mast—were forced down by the mainsail. None of them made it back to the surface. Bill and I were thrown clear of the boat by some miracle. Tommy, the deckhand, was trapped in his cabin.

We later learned that a newborn mountaintop had reared up like a giant's fist to catch hold of our keel. Our forward momentum sent the bow straight down. Life rafts and safety vests were useless—there'd been no time. Bill and I were lucky. The crew of a schooner several hundred yards to starboard saw the whole thing and picked us up.

Shit happens even on the most perfect of days.

Acknowledgments

So many writer friends who have helped me with critiques of different stories in this collection. A couple of these stories date all the way back to workshops at The Wynne Home in Huntsville, Texas. Thanks to Linda Pease and the City of Huntsville for allowing my creative writing MFA cohort, led by Scott Kaukonen, to meet there once a week. The cohort included Matthew Bennett, Reina Shay Broussard, Kari Lee Bush, Eric Ellsworth, Jake Gebhardt, Cody Michael Harrison, Gary Horton, Kimberlee Rayl Slaughter, Brian McWilliams, Chris Mitchell, Nathan Ridings, and Olivia Strand. I also participated in a student-led workshop at that time organized by Julian Kindred, with Eduardo de Luna, Heather Robbins Marti, Cora Davis, and Nathan Ridings among others who came and went less often. These were first to hear some of the shorter pieces.

More recent critique partners include Jodi Angel, Siobhan Wright, and Jen Knox, with whom I participated in generative workshops. I must offer special thanks to Luanne Smith for inviting me to the Woodbridge Writers Workshop where I got to work with Richard Bauch, Jill McCorkle, and Connie Mae Fowler as faculty. And to Michael Simms and Mike Hilbig who both read this manuscript multiple times. Thanks always to the best proof-reader among us, Elizabeth Evans. And finally, to my accountability group, who listen to me grumble and offer encouragement weekly. They remind me to keep on using this writing tool I've been given. They are Amanda Skenandore, Windy Wimmer, Veronica Klash, and Tonya Todd.

And I mustn't forget the wonderful staff at Cornerstone Press who have worked with me on this final version, led by Dr. Ross Tangedal, with managing editor Karlie Harpold. They have made this whole publishing process so easy. And thanks also to Sam Bjork, Sophie McPherson, Maddie Schultz, and Autumn Vine in media/sales.

* * *

Some of the stories in this collection have been previously published or placed in competitions. Many thanks to the editors of these literary journals and judges in these competitions who first saw merit in the work.

"Bracketville, Texas, 1964." *Flare: The Flagler Review.* (2020). This story also placed in the NYC Midnight Flash Fiction Contest in 2019.

"Chumming for Sharks," *The Helix Magazine* (2017). This story also placed in the NYC Midnight Short Story Challenge (2016).

"Do You Know the Bunny Hop?" *époque press*, "Illumination" issue. (2019).

"The Magic Airplane," *Sad Girls Club Literary Blog*, January 26, 2021.

"Nebula and the Wolf," *Writing Texas*, edited by Laurence Musgrove, Vol.8, 2021-2022.

"A Simple Twist of Fate," *Kestrel*, Issue 43, Summer 2020.

"Shit Happens" winner of the Cracked Flash Fiction June 14, 2017.

"Strings of Solace," JerryJazzMusician.com (2019).

"Trust Issues," quarter finalist, 2021 ScreenCraft Cinematic Short Story Competition Quarterfinalists, January 6, 2021.

KIMBERLY PARISH (K.P.) DAVIS was once upon a time an adrenaline junkie. Director and founder of Madville Publishing, Kim grew up in Texas, but sailed around the world as a chef aboard private yachts for fifteen years before returning home. Her short fiction, nonfiction, and poetry have been published in literary journals, anthologies, and online.